D0852949

TRULUCK

SawRed

ALSO BY BOB TRULUCK

Street Level (2000)

SawRed

NEW HANOVER COUNTY
PUBLIC LIBRARY
201 CHESTNUT STREET
WILMINGTON, NC 28401

A MYSTERY

BOB TRULUCK

20 03

Dennis McMillan Publications

Saw Red copyright © 2003 by Bob Truluck.
All rights reserved.

FIRST EDITION
Published August 2003

Dustjacket and interior artwork
by Michael Kellner.

ISBN 0-939767-45-7 (cloth binding)
ISBN 0-939767-46-5 (quarter-morocco binding)

Dennis McMillan Publications
4460 N. Hacienda del Sol (Guest House)
Tucson, Arizona 85718   Tel. (520)-529-6636
http://www.dennismcmillan.com

To Leslie who always believes I can do this,
even when I think I can't.
You're from a Buick 6 and I love you.

It is not funny that a man should be killed,
but it is sometimes funny that he should be
killed for so little, and that his death should
be the coin of what we call civilization.

from The Simple Art of Murder
by Raymond Chandler

Baby, if ya wanna get low
Baby, if ya wanna get high
It makes no sense at all
I saw red
I saw red
One more secret lover that
I shot dead

from Saw Red
by Bradley Nowell/Sublime

ACKNOWLEDGMENTS

Thanks to my wife/typist/personal-motivator
and her tolerance.
Thanks to Chuck Anthony for making me
loook literitt.
Thanks to my mom for not reading my books
and telling Jesus on me.
Thanks to my dad for not letting my mom read
my books.
Thanks to Florida for being itself.
Thanks to the independent booksellers.
Thanks to my brothers and sisters in this craft.

Thanks to *everybody* who gets it. You're my
peeps and I love you.

—Bob

SawRed

DISCLAIMER

Nothing contained herein is intended to represent anything beyond pulp-trash and/or pop-fiction. This material has been produced for entertainment purposes only. Intentional misuse of this product, as with any form of disposable literature, could result in mental, physical or spiritual injury. The reader should further indemnify and hold harmless the author for any enlightenment gained from this material. It is the author's opinion that any such occurrence would be the result of misuse or, more likely, pure accident. Enjoy.

— Author

ONE

The first time I laid eyes on Terry Sebring she was showing me the pussy in a hotel bar. I didn't take it personally or any other way really. I just saw it as some damned good advertising about the same old thing. I guess that's how I took it. Our paths crossed again the next morning. Briefly. The elevator, same joint. That time I was noticing she had a decent sense of humor and spoke casual French. I had already noticed she was a knockout redhead.

I thought about her, our small encounter, a couple of times, then put it where stuff like that goes. I didn't think any more about her until a year or two later when she knocked on my front door to remind me. And I knew she had trouble. Seems nobody knocks on my door unless they've got trouble. It's that kind of door.

I was looking at working-girl, day-off. Fine-gauge sweater thing the nancy-name people might call wheat or something like that. Tan worked. Almost-white linen skirt tickling the bottoms of her kneecaps. Some classy gold stuff at her neck, an emerald not much bigger than a thumbnail on one hand. Plain brown Mary Janes, strap and all, that would have set you back a bill and a half, easy. A soft leather bag, brown to match the shoes, slung across a shoulder. Curb appeal for days.

Passing her on the street, not knowing any better, not knowing she was a high-dollar whore, you'd think money.

Not pretend money like the assholes up in Winter Park or the phony fucks out in the burbs; the McCoy. The kind that actually comes with some class attached.

Odd how class is almost never encountered where you'd expect it, but, like game or something, it pops up in the most unusual places. Terry Sebring had plenty of both. The class was out there, obvious. The game I would have bet on.

It took me a moment to place her and my mouth was in forward motion but didn't have a name for her. I rolled with it. "'Sup, Red? You lost?"

"Not anymore, private dick Sloan. How have you been?" I'd forgotten the voice, how it roused something down low. Something about 20 million years old. Something that would have made Odysseus gnaw both arms off.

I threw out a shrug, turned it into a *mi-casa-su-casa* gesture with a free hand. We left the sunshine outside for the tourists and she glanced around my short digs while I shut the door. She didn't look impressed.

"Cute."

Too bad that wasn't what I was going for. "Thanks. Pull up a chair." She did, and I offered her something to drink if she wasn't looking for much more than beer or iced tap water. She said no and I plopped in an old chair I never sit in. I remembered why.

The Terry Sebring who knocked on my door had been putting out the smile, the come-on number, an indispensable accessory in her racket, I'm sure. I had been getting the smile but not much else. Now, sitting here, recataloguing each other, her eyes, the ones so green you wanted to ask her if they were contacts, were glittering like the first time we met. She'd been laughing at me then, and I was betting she was laughing at me now. I sat tight, waiting to get to the small talk.

Short wait. "Are you staying busy?"

I shrugged. "At times." I was busy like a pickpocket at a nudist joint. "How about you? You keeping the old dance card filled?" It wasn't that funny.

She smiled anyway. "Actually, no. I've been working the market more than the four-stars lately. The way things are jumping around on Wall Street right now, I can really manage some nice surprises if I stay on top of it. Play the short side occasionally." I got the eyes and a shrug. "I always seem to do my best work on the supply side."

That meant about zip to me. I keep most of my portfolio in my sock drawer. "I don't even know your name. Do I need to?"

"Terry Sebring. Are you curious how I ended up at your front door?"

"Yeah, I'm curious."

"I asked a couple of vice cops I know. They knew you."

"I know some vice cops?"

"Chick Rappaport?"

"Yeah. I know Chick."

"Freddie Paulk?"

"Yeah. I know Freddie too." I guess I did know some vice cops. "They know where I live?"

"No. And your phone is unlisted. You could be in the witness relocation program."

No I couldn't.

"They put me in touch with a Lieutenant Detective Booker."

"Good old Booker." Mose Booker was the nearest thing to a friend I had over at the sheriff's department. Still, a tenuous relationship on a good day.

"The lieutenant's partner, a Detective Channing, called back instead. He didn't have your number but he gave me directions."

"Good old Channing." I got a free smile with that one.

3

"I take it you and Channing aren't friends."

"We share a mutual disrespect." I was being a nice boy. I hated his fucking guts and he mine. "He give me a glowing recommendation?"

Her funny eyebrows said it. "No." Pause. "Are you gay?"

"No." The harmonics I was putting on it were right out of junior high. What I recovered with wasn't that far from school-yard shit anyway. "I wouldn't put much stock in what Channing says. Nobody else does. If that's where this is coming from."

Terry shrugged some nice shoulders. "That and the first night we met? The offer you refused?"

I was grinning at the memory. "Yeah. I recall. Like I said then, sweetheart, there's no such thing as a freebie. I still believe it."

"I think there's a little more to it than that." She was laughing at me with her eyes again.

My head went sideways, cousin to a nod, cousin to a shrug thing. "Could be."

"You know, to be putting out such a hip image, you tend to be a little old-fashioned."

I didn't really think I was putting out a hip image. I don't always tuck my shirttail in. Maybe that was what she was talking about. "Probably more than I'd like to admit. You come over here to ask me why I didn't take the freebie?"

4

TWO

The smile went away and I watched the so green eyes go aquamarine on me. "No."

Terry brought out the purse and fussed around in it until she found an envelope. The purse went away and her hands floated to her knees with the envelope.

"People call you Duncan?"

I smiled like Mona Lisa was my mother. "People call me all sorts of things. How 'bout you?"

Terry picked up the smile, did a better job with it, said, "You look more like a Sloan."

"Then make it Sloan."

She nodded, falling back into herself a bit. "Someone's trashing my business, Sloan."

I hashed that around for a beat or two. First thought: Would I need a red crushed-velvet suit? A hat with a medium-sized feather? A Caddy with a metal flake paint job?

"By 'someone' you mean you don't know who?"

"Yes. I assume it's connected to the guys who stole my car."

One back loop was enough. "Maybe you should start from the beginning."

"I think so." The envelope came in my direction. "You may need this."

I opened the envelope and retrieved a couple of triple-folded sheets. Up first, a copy of a title: new Jaguar. Next was a list, eighteen names with phone numbers. I didn't need Nostradamus to figure that one.

"You drive a Jag?" It wasn't important; I was just amusing myself.

"Yes—I did, until about three weeks ago. I ran inside a store to return something, came out and two guys were getting in my car. I got to watch them drive out of the parking lot."

"You get a good look at them?" It really didn't matter.

A shrug and a flick of the eyebrows. "I saw mostly hair." She made motions beside her head with her hands. "A mullet-cut? and a blond spike thing."

"You report this?"

"Yes. I went back in the shop and called the police."

"The cops had no luck?" I knew the answer.

"No."

"Your dance card in the car?"

"Yes. My Palm Pilot."

"And now someone's squeezing your customers?"

"Exactly. I've had several of them call." The face she had to go with it said the conversations weren't pretty.

"Has he got around to squeezing *you* yet?"

"No. And I hear what you're saying. I've been expecting it too. Can you find him first?"

I knew where I was going next, but I sat on it, make it look like I was thinking about it. Before I started looking dull, I said, "Couple of things. A car title and a list of names aren't much of a start. Say I'm lucky enough to find out who's on first. I do what? Go see the guy? Straighten him out? Beat him up? Break his legs? What? None of that sounds like something a guy without a good health plan would touch. And I hardly ever shoot anybody weekdays anymore."

Terry started to speak and I raised an interrupting finger. "And second, I'm having a little trouble with a jackboy coming

6

up with the gray matter to even *see* a trick in there, much less get on with it. So there's a wild card in the game somewhere and wild cards make me nervous.

"Here's what I think: there's more to this story than I'm hearing. Maybe you know that part, maybe you don't. Maybe it's my suspicious nature, but I think it has more to do with you coming here on a referral from Chick Rap and Freddie Paulk. These guys aren't Starsky and Hutch. They're in a rough trade and they play for keeps. So they tell you I play hardball, and you don't know what you need, but you figure somebody like me might come closer to doing whatever it takes than the guys with some carpeted square footage and a few file cabinets. It's pretty duh simple. You've got big troubles, sister. I'm thinking if this somebody didn't have the potential to get your arm up behind your back, you wouldn't be sitting here. How am I doing so far?"

"Pretty good." She was giving me a sharp look.

I gave her a piece of a nod. "Something else that jumps out at me. I'm looking around and the only people I see with problems are right here." I waved the list of names. "I can't see you all that committed to any of these guys, and why you wouldn't simply cut bait and run bothers hell out of me. I'm sure you've got your reasons, they just don't seem real logical. But we'll let that go for now.

"All that considered, I think you came to the right place, but I need to hear all of it, particularly the part that makes me feel good about turning this guy out for you. That's what *I* need. So if you won't, or can't, get off the rest of it, I'm not interested." I let that float around out there, added: "That's how people get hurt. In my business, it can even get you dead without ever seeing it coming." I stood on it for another beat, said, "So either give it up, and I mean all of it, or sit on the rest. I don't wanna hear it." I gave her a nice smile. "You decide." I'd said plenty, now we'd see if she could talk me into it.

The eyes were nailing me, looking down in there, rummaging around. Maybe she found what she was looking for. She said, "I would be putting a lot of trust in someone I hardly know."

I didn't know how I was supposed to field that. I could have pointed out how she came to my door. Unsolicited. I said, "Sorry. I don't have what you might call references. Most everyone I service also requires discretion." I threw out a pair of innocent hands. "Lookit where I live. Do I look like I'm real successful at getting money outta people?"

She did the Mona Lisa for me. "No. And the references from Freddie and Chick are sufficient. They said you were good. I know them well enough to know that's a high compliment. Chick said you even did time protecting a client once."

"That's bullshit. I did time for not ratting out two guys from Jersey with loud suits and cheap loafers. That's an altogether different situation. But your average day? No, I can't start crying every time the cops go for short and curly. I did, I couldn't go on hanging shingle in this burg for long. Like I say, most of my trade is of the discreet variety. But if it gets hot enough, bet your ass I'll give it up. I don't mind sitting in Orange County's facility on Thirty-third Street for a night or two first, see how sincere they are."

Terry was laughing at me. "You're serious, aren't you?"

"Sure. For a night or two. After that?" I was shrugging. "Keep in mind, I gotta live with the cops too. So if this thing goes to shit, we'll have no privileged confidentiality. Unless you've got a lawyer and I'm working for him. It comes to it, I can arrange that. Even retroactive, should the need arise."

She wasn't listening. The details weren't where she was

8

finding the devil. She was back inside me, looking around again. Back out, a little Zen breath to relax, throw an excellent leg on an excellent knee, look at the finger with the slab of emerald balanced on it. "You know, you don't look that dependable."

"Yeah, I know. I don't look so smart either."

"But you are."

It should have been a question, but it wasn't, and I didn't really get it. I shrugged out a sure.

The eyes were back to the color of the emerald and she laughed at me with them some. "I think I heard something about a beer?"

I got up and knocked the caps off a couple of Newcastles, got her a CD cover for a coaster, and tried another chair. I really needed to invest a couple of dollars in some decent furniture.

Terry did the Zen breath thing again, preluding the final act, I hoped. "Okay, Sloan, and this is just guessing. I don't know any of this for certain."

I could have given her a little bump with something clever, like: Can anyone ever really know anything? But shit that heavy makes my brain hemorrhage. I opted for: "That's all I'm looking for, Red."

"I think someone on the list is involved. I don't see how that could be possible, but nothing else explains this." Another purse search, another envelope, another face read. She pushed it at me.

The secret *samadhi* was half a dozen photographs of Terry in work clothes at different cocktail lounges, smiling for dollars with guys who looked like they wouldn't mind spending a few bucks on a nice piece like Terry Sebring. I flipped through them while I asked what made her think one of her boys had turned cannibalistic, started eating the others.

9

"Sloan, I'm harder to find than you are. I don't just pick up clients in bars at random."

My arched eyebrows and my cynical mouth begged to differ. They were thinking about the show at the Hilton she'd done for me a couple of years back. "You know, I could mount a decent argument against that statement." That time, Terry had dropped a move on me I'm sure is as old as boys and girls hanging around the watering hole. I got to see what happens when someone with no panties and a short skirt doesn't mind her manners, forgets to watch her knees. Like I say, I'd thought it was advertising. I got straightened out.

Terry wagged her head back and forth over a nice smile. "Do you really think you look like a guy who could afford five hundred an hour? And don't you think the bishop ever says a prayer when he's not doing mass?"

Hmm. We might have to get back to that some other time. "You feel like the snaps were taken by someone who knew where to find you?"

"Absolutely. But how? No way my name or address were in or on that PalmPilot. Unless you came in on a referral, no way could you find me."

"How did you come by these?"

"They were in my mailbox yesterday."

"No note?"

"No."

I looked through them again. "And what else don't you know for certain?"

Terry found a dose and a half of air while my eyes watched what it did to her chest, watched it raise her breasts and tighten the sweater. I might've sat there all day and watched but she said, "And I think someone else on the list is having big problems with being outed. To the point I'm a little scared. No. That's not right. I'm a *lot* scared."

The eyes testified in favor of her fear. "My apartment in Buena Vista's been burgled twice, and someone is following me. I think."

I was pretty sure the last was attached to the being-followed part. "Could it be the boys who took the Jag?" We should be so lucky.

Her head dipped and went left to right a couple of times. "No. These people are more serious. Dark suits and cowboy hats. I've seen them twice, and they sit and stare like –I don't know, Sloan, like I could already be dead. It makes me think they're just waiting for the right moment. Creepy guys."

I allowed that to bounce around inside my skull a little. "You think they followed you here?"

I could tell she hadn't even thought about it. Now that she did, it bothered her. "I guess they could have."

"Chick and Freddie couldn't talk to them?"

She was smiling at my smarts. "No. You're right; I asked them to. When they were watching, the guys would vanish. Like they knew or something."

That bothered me much. About the only vermin with that kind of savvy and instinct were clippers. Professional clippers. "What did Chick and Freddie say?"

"They said I needed to find some . . . I think they called it 'private talent'."

"That's when my name came up?"

"Yes."

"They say anything else? About your fan club?"

"No. Only you should know how to deal with it."

"You own a handgun?"

"No. Should I get one?"

I shook my head. "Nah. Semi-law-abiding citizens like you and me, it takes three days to do the do. By that time this thing may be over. I'll loan you something. Can you shoot?"

11

The better question was: Would you shoot? But nobody can answer that one until it comes to scratch.

"Well enough. I grew up on a farm outside Winter Haven." The eyes watched me, seeing how smart I really was.

"You're one of those Sebrings?"

"Yes, Sloan, one of those Sebrings. Nobody's happy about it, but we're all stuck with it. Don't hold it against me, all right?"

The Sebrings I had overlooked had been growing oranges in Florida about a hundred years, buying land the whole time. A few years back, they owned about half of the sandy nothingness between Orlando and Cypress Gardens. When someone from California imagined up a theme park out there, the Sebrings were accelerated from solid land-rich, money-poor fruit farmers to instant meganaires. You could still smell the ink on the money. It ruined them to the extent that the name had become synonymous with family infighting, treachery, greed, and bumpkins-with-new-money in general. Seems like there was more, like a murder or an attempt or two. I couldn't call it up right now.

"Should I let it go?"

Terry shrugged. "It doesn't matter. Not anymore. I haven't seen any of them in years." She took a sip of beer and touched her lips with the crook of a finger.

"There's no way this is connected to them, is there?"

"I don't see how." She was lying. We both could see how.

All of a sudden this thing had more fuzzy characters than a first novel. Must have sounded like my kind of fun. I excused myself and went out to my car.

In my old 'Vette, stuffed in a ripped-out seam of the carpet, there's a little .32-cal Berretta in a zip-lock baggy. If you asked me anything about it, I wouldn't know shit. It's not registered to me and I have no idea how it got there. I brought it in, racked one under the pin, and sat it on the table. "There's a thumb-latch safety below the slide, seven pills ready to party. You need to use it, drop all seven. You got somewhere to lay dogo for a couple of days?"

Terry didn't even have to think about it. "Yes. Does this mean you're going to help me?"

"Maybe. Back to question one. What do you expect me to do when I find the greedy party?" I didn't want to think too much about what it was going to take to deal with the other team, the guys in hats.

No forethought needed again. "I want you to pay him."

I could feel my eyes rolling and my lips pursed against a noisy exhale. "You know better than that, Terry. You'd just be paying rent. Six months, the guy's back."

I got a face without any come-and-get-it involved. The business face, I guess.

"Then I'll pay him again. Look, Sloan, I run a quiet shop. High-end, repeat business. I do very well and have access to incredible insider tidbits that allow me to do much better than the average trader. Trust me, that alone almost makes it worth it."

We traded looks over that. I had to say it. "Almost?"

We held the stare; she said, "Sloan, let's don't get over there, how about it?"

I gave her a smile and a head shake I'm sure she'd seen before. A hundred times.

"When I find the guy and you pay him, I'll toss Booker or Chick and Freddie on him. If he's smart he'll take his pork and roll on up the street."

"And if he's not?"

"Then I guess I'll have to go see him. Break his legs."

The eyes had gone back to emerald and they flared in amusement. "You think you can find him?"

13

I shrugged for her. "Sure. I'll find the guys who took the car, ask them nice to tell me who they sold your book to."

"The police couldn't find them."

I shook my head. "The cops weren't looking for them. They were looking for the car."

"And you can find them?"

"Or the car. Same thing. I'll find them, unless they're island boys. That's a very private club. The hairdos, they don't sound Jamaican or Hispanic."

"No. They appeared to be fairly indigenous."

"Not a problem, then. Where did this go down? The car thing?"

"A strip mall in Winter Park."

"Easier still." My end of town. "Okay, listen. When you leave, go north on the Trail. Cross the southbound and pull in at the naughty-movie joint on the left. Pretend your lipstick needs adjusting or something. Give it a minute and a half, then haul your ass to wherever it is you can hide out. And stay there."

"Do you think you can make this go away?"

I thought about it a second, couldn't see the answer, so I answered another question that hadn't really been asked. "Yeah. I'll find your guy."

"You'll need money." A quick statement preceding a now-familiar search in the purse. "What am I looking at, ratewise?"

"High."

She came out with a nice manila envelope this time. "I heard."

"Channing?"

"Everybody."

I thought about that. "Good. Five grand up front. Win, loose, draw, you're out the five. And that could just be starters. I'll

14

let you know when it's gone. And I don't do accounting work. You need a tax deduction, find a charity. What else?"

Terry was doing a virtual laugh. No sound, but plenty of amusement. "That's probably the sorriest sales pitch I've ever heard. Here, I'll take a double." A couple of bundles of dough hit the table.

"Deal?"

"Deal."

"Aren't you going to count it?"

"I did when it hit the table, sweetheart."

THREE

Terry left and I gave her a couple of blocks' head start. On the way out the door, I grabbed the Smith & Wesson 9-millimeter that usually lives in my kitchen cabinet. I gave the neighbors a break, shoved it down the front of my pants. I couldn't see making them jealous, me walking around with a fifteen-shot handgun and all they're packing is weed whackers and leaf blowers.

I jammed around the back way to what's proudly touted as the world's biggest smut depot, the Fairvilla Megastore. Tools, accessories, how-to videos and manuals, battery chargers, and *potions d'amour*. A place about nothing but getting freaky. From your no-shit hard-core to whimsical novelty.

Across the street a black Lincoln squatted in front of a warehouse. The Lincoln was in a strange spot, backed into an unemployed drive at a locked gate. I looked again and saw two cowboy hats inside. Terry was doing kissy lips at the mirror when I rode by and acted like I didn't know her.

The Lincoln began to move and I had to scare shit out of a guy in a big produce truck to make it across the two busy northbound lanes. Scared shit out of me too, but it looked good when I careened around and blocked the car's exit.

The cowboys inside weren't Mensa material and it took them a few seconds to recall how a car a lot like mine was in the drive where the object of their recent affections had spent the last hour. It was enough seconds that I had my feet on the tarmac with the Smith in hand.

The cat on the passenger side went looking for something under his left arm so I quick-dropped a couple of caps between their heads. The windshield evaporated and so did the cowboys.

Their lack of presence didn't stop the Lincoln from jumping on reverse at about ninety. The punch took them through the chain-link gate and they might have ended up in Daytona if it hadn't been for a cinder-block loading dock.

The racket got us a spectator, a guy from the warehouse. He walked out on the dock the Lincoln had snuggled against and took a good look at the situation. Then he looked over at me standing there with the gat hanging. I waved my free hand, said, "How's it going, brother?"

He grinned pretty good and said, "Better'n these boys. How 'bout you?"

"Been better. See you around."

He agreed like we'd probably all do this again real soon, and I walked back to my car.

I could see Terry's car was getting smaller up Orange Blossom Trail as I popped my door. Before I folded myself to get in, the warehouse guy called out: "Hey, you a cop or something?"

I would have probably fit somewhere under the *or something,* but the warehouseman was having such fun the way it was breaking, I let it ride. I shook my head. "Nope."

We grinned at each other for a few beats, then he said, "Awright. Should I call nine-one-one?"

"Whatever flips your pancakes, big man."

My rearview told me he was still grinning as I wedged in the rush. Hey, out here on the Trail, seeing a guy blasting a shiny black Lincoln with a shiny black handgun ain't nothing but a thang. Maybe we would all do it again sometime.

17

FOUR

A couple of blocks north, I jumped out of the cattle drive, circled back around to the crib. I sat in the afternoon nothing for a while with my feet kicked up on Terry Sebring's dough. It didn't inspire me but it was entertaining that I thought it might.

Trying to think about nothing is a trick the mechanics of the brain won't support, but it almost always flushes up some interesting shit. Some of it can even be pertinent.

I wondered some about Terry and her family. That part could have been being nosy, but I didn't think so. Somehow, it could end up in the mix. Terry thought so too. If she didn't, she wouldn't have planted the seed. Maybe it was nothing more than a warning about blundering over into high cotton. Who knows?

The part that still bothered me most was why Terry didn't just duck and run. I didn't buy, even momentarily, that she was particularly scared of the two boys who were following her. She wouldn't be scared of anybody. She could have handled these guys, this situation, as represented to date to me.

The list being on the street was a consideration. Someone was, no doubt, poised to commit some pretty persuasion, but like I had told her, that consideration was based solely on the iffy premise Terry gave a fuck what happened to the names on the list. I knew I didn't.

And the ten big fish Terry was willing to toss at me would have gotten the guy doing the squeezing an easy thirty in barter. I was hard-pressed to believe it hadn't crossed her mind. Even if the deal was temporary, it would have bought enough time she could change habits and rebuild her list. God knows the world's full of rich guys looking for pussy.

She wanted me to believe she was concerned about losing her connection to stock market secrets. That was bullshit. She was a smart cookie, smart enough that it seemed more likely Terry could give as good as she could get in that arena.

And that part of me she had labeled old-fashioned belabored the issue of why someone that smart and successful still pedaled her ass on the open market. I was sure that I was just being nosy there, but it still bothered hell out of me. Goddam it, everything about the woman bothered me, bothered me in a spot I couldn't reach to scratch. Circle around, Sloan; don't step in the hole, son.

Back to business. This guy, the squeezer, had somehow disturbed a bed of snakes. If I pinned him quick, maybe the snakes in the Lincoln would go away. I warned myself not to underestimate this guy. I was preconceiving him as some middle-aged yuppie and I knew I could be so wrong. Another hole to keep a foot out of.

Maybe the lux footstool had inspired me after all. Maybe it was a couple more Newcastles I nibbled. Maybe I had a bad reaction from mixing alcohol and sudden wealth.

I topped off the clip in my piece, grabbed a spare rack and went to find a couple of fairly indigenous white boys liked to steal cars, fuck their day up.

FIVE

Charlie Boscoe's a hell of a mechanic and would probably do an incredible legit business if the public could find him.

Charlie Boscoe doesn't have any more inclination to be in the public eye than he does to enjoy legitimate business. If it's legal, Charlie doesn't need it. What fun is that? Where's the art?

And Missus Boscoe's baddest baby boy is indeed the artist. Charlie could sell you your own car *à la carte* fifteen minutes after you park it and you'd never have a clue. He's good at what he does.

Don't get me wrong. Charlie's no car thief. Anymore, anyhow. He started out that route several years back but drifted over to a strictly piece-out deal. Parts-on-demand stuff. Not exactly a legal trade but I still admired him for at least partially rehabilitating himself without putting the state of Florida to any particular trouble or expense.

He keeps a few straight customers for the tax man, people he's known since jump and who don't mind where he makes his spending money. You might even see a cop in there getting his pickup revamped on the cheap. I don't ask questions. That's why me and Charlie stay friends. That and the fact I always pay cash.

Charlie and I go back so far I don't even remember how I met him. Has to be twelve, fourteen years, and the bastard looks exactly the same. Five-eight, five-nine. Barrel-chested, thick-limbed, just enough fat to smooth him down, unrip him some. And a head of hair Geronimo would have killed for. It begins at a widow's peak over a couple of brown buttons and hangs down his back in a ponytail. He might be a merry doughboy but for those buttons. One message in the eyes: I own where I'm standing and you don't.

Charlie pulls a lot of water in his world, and a guy like me can stand a guy like Charlie Boscoe. If it's got wheels and it's gotten lost, he's a good place to start.

Besides, I'm a guy that drives a plastic car that was stamped out while Gerry Ford was falling off airplanes and beaning taxpayers with golf balls. I need a Charlie Boscoe worse than I need a handful of coat hangers and a roll of fresh duct tape. More than that, friends of Charlie's can be pretty sure of waking up 365 with their shit in the driveway. If not, you can call Charlie and it'll turn back up like a bad habit by morning.

There's an old citrus house on the north Trail that woke up one day and found itself surrounded by perfect rows of houses instead of orange trees. With no shame whatsoever, it jumped the wall and became a recycling joint. The one-man's-trash theory seemed to work, and if there's something Orlando's got its share of, it's trash. And by God, if Uncle Wally has taught us Florida crackers anything, it's if you got lemons, open a lemonade stand.

In a back corner, where pieces of yesterday's news rally and roll like tumbleweeds, is four or five thousand feet of tin building where Doctor Boscoe does the dissecting.

I dodged potholes and recycle bins and semis to this modern version of the hole-in-the-wall and saw the crack of Charlie's ass peeping out of his jeans while he stuck his head under a hood. It wasn't pretty. Nothing here is but the lightening-fast paint jobs zipped out in the last bay.

Charlie straightened, put out the trademark scowl, saw it

was me and put the scowl back under the hood. I found some vacant sand and shut my ride down, walked over and stood behind Charlie. He did a nine-point-five on ignoring me for a few, then said to the engine, "You got a vacuum leak," but it was meant for me.

I grinned at the half-moon rising. "And you could tell? Me just pulling in here?"

Charlie surfaced with a distributor, wires dangling. It looked like a dead mechanical octopus. "I could tell from across the street. Why'on't you go ahead, get that thing crushed you ain't gone do no better by it, Sloan."

"I did, you'd be out half your yearly taxable income. Got a minute?"

The scowl collapsed into something painful, suspicion screwing up his whole face. "Oh shit," to me; to a guy coming out of bay number two with a transmission on a shoulder: "Hey, Shiny, fuck-off's working. Get the Polaroid."

Shiny was Charlie's Pancho, affable to a fault, big as a grasshopper and almost as hairy. "Hey, Sloan. How's it hanging?" He topped it with a goofed-up grin, showing me how several years of sucking on the glass pipe will melt your front teeth for you. A smarter guy might even wonder what it was doing to the frontal lobes.

"A little to the left, Shiny, little to the left. How 'bout you?"

"Same old same-old. Workin' for assholes, what's gonna change?" The transmission on his shoulder probably weighed more than Shiny did. The strain on his face, it could have been made out of plastic instead of good *De*-troit cast.

"I hear you when you talking to me, baby. Don't get any on you." I tossed it over my shoulder as I followed Charlie to his office.

Charlie worked on his hands with a rag until he got to the

door, turned, said, "Come on, dipshit. I ain't got all day to play around with the local gentry."

I shook my head and followed him inside.

The inside of Charlie's office is entirely papered in pinup shit, most from parts-and-supplies vendors. The amazing thing about it, although there's enough testosterone floating around the place to grow hair on Aphrodite's back, thanks to strategic placement of various props there's not a nip or a muff in the crowd. Go figure that. I moved a black jacket with a big red 3, a cell phone and a bearing set off the only spare chair and couldn't find a free spot to put the stuff except my lap. Maybe Charlie liked clutter.

Charlie was leaning over the office phone punching caller ID, emphasizing each punch with stuff like: asshole, dipshit, fuckhead. Talking nice about his customers. The phone rang, Charlie checked the ID, picked it up. Instead of hi, hello, how are you, the caller got, "You come up with my three seventy-five?" Pause to listen. "The fuck you callin' here, then?" Racked the phone. "Asshole's been owin' me three seventy-five for six months and got the balls to call here lookin' for sump'm else. On credit. Dickheads. Whatcha need, Sloan?"

"Well, hey, Charlie. How you been? Yeah, I been fine too, thanks." I grinned, sat the junk from my lap on top of some other clutter on Charlie's desk. "You talk about me like that when I'm not around?"

Charlie looked at me and grinned. "You're a fuckin' mess, Sloan." The grin evaporated like it was made of dry ice. "You did want something, right?"

"You ever see me when I didn't?"

He thought about it. "Nah. That's what I like about you. That and the fact you understand what 'cash only' means," putting up two fingers and rubbing in a clichéd move. "Shoot."

"Black Jag sedan. Nearly new. Ran away from home with a couple of white boys three weeks back. You seen?"

Charlie stared through me, squinting one eye, remembering. He leaned to the phone, nabbed the handpiece and fed it numbers.

"Hey. Black Jag. Two weeks back you called." Pause. "Yeah? Well I'll just give that boy a call."

He dropped the connect, said, "Getting closer." More numbers were punched. We did that twice again, and I heard: "Un-huh. And it's still settin' there?" Pause. "One piece?" Pause. "Good. I owe you a Co-Cola."

I got some deadpan. "You still living in College Park?"

"Yeah."

He nodded. "You coulda throwed a rock and hit it from your place. Shady Grady. The limo place on Edgewater." More deadpan. "Tell me you ain't sunk to havin' to chase runaway cars. Please."

I grinned while I peeled off one of Terry's hundreds, creased it longways, and dropped it on the gridlock that was Charlie's desktop. "Not yet."

I got the good-old-boy grin again. "Good. You got me curious, though."

"Charlie, you were a curious motherfucker first time I met you. Don't change on account of me."

"You ain't gone tell me why you want the Jag, are you?"

I put a head wag on a frown. "Nope."

Charlie studied me a few, said, "Grady wears a Colt thirty-eight in his left boot."

My turn to grin. "He prone to pull it?"

Charlie's head was nodding slowly as the phone rang. Maybe nobody heard it. A few rings, Charlie's answering machine kicked in, the caller killed it. "Yeah. Fucker looks like Elvis and thinks he's Clint Eastwood. You watch 'im."

24

I figured Terry wouldn't mind me not getting popped, so I gave him another one of her C-notes. "Thanks for the heads-up."

"Like I said, you understand the importance of cash money. A rare quality in the unmotivated."

I'm sure I'd have garnered even greater compliments, but the phone squawked again. Charlie checked the little screen, said, "Fuckhead," and nabbed the business end. "You got my seven hundred? The fuck you callin' here for, then? Yeah? Well, that and a five-dollar bill'll get you a fancy cup o' coffee over at Starbucks. Call me back when you start payin' your bills, dickhead." Pause. "Oh yeah? Well my ass'll be right here, you get to feelin' froggy."

There was more, but I shut the door on it, caught Shiny under my hood. He had a length of vacuum hose, trading it for one the same size that had gone to the consistency of raw squid.

"There you go, Mr. Sloan. That oughta double your gas mileage." Shiny gave me his idiot's grin. "You know your motor oil looks like pitch? You oughta treat this old lady better, Sloan."

"Yeah, that's what I keep hearing, but you know what happens. You treat 'em good, they run off with the pool boy."

"Sounds like you know somethin' 'bout that. You still batchin' it?"

"Damn straight, Shiny. You?"

"Hell, yeah. Won't nobody have me."

"My excuse too. See you, hoss."

Shiny shut my hood like it was Waterford and I hammered across the lot, skinning rubber off my rears. Hanging here always does something crazy to your nuts, makes you act out worse than a juke with a homemade pistol.

SIX

A-Aardvark Limousine Service. You had to give it to the owner. He was strong on marketing, if a little short in the imagination department. I'd have bet one of Terry's hundred-dollar bills his outfit was dead top in the yellow pages. If not, he'd add another *A*.

The joint was, no doubt, born as a full-service gas station. Yet another case of shameless identity lane-changing in a boomtown. A childless pump island still held on, supports rising for the required overhang of its past life. Turquoise-and-white now. A cute little aardvark in a chauffeur's cap duplicated here and there lest you forgot where you were.

For all the comings and goings, the resident anteaters could have been in hibernation. A few stretched-out Caddies were lined up neatly, but no aardvarks in sight.

It was close to four o'clock and I was next door at a mom-and-pop outfit sporting another imaginative name. The Dairy King. Catholic girls in plaid skirts from the parochial high school across the street were practicing their profanity while I gnawed on a couple of Coneys. The dogs might have been older than the apprentice profaners.

After a bit of whispering and shot glances, one of the girls came up, leaned over and placed her hands on the top of the concrete table I was using. I noticed her white shirt was unbuttoned, post last bell I'm sure. Past any venial point the sisters would have tolerated. She gave me what I guessed was the current version of the *eye* and asked, "You got a dollar I can have?"

I took a big bite off the mature Coney, chewed it awhile. My eyes tried not to look down her shirt. I'm sure she was disappointed. "You know, little girls that play around with big, grown-up men sometimes end up with their pictures on milk cartons." I looked up and put as fatherly a smile as I own on my face.

It put a piece of a sneer on her fresh face and she said, "That's bullshit."

"That's nice talk. You need money, go ask your daddy for an advance on your allowance."

A flush came up from the over-opened shirt, took her face. I thought for a moment she was appropriately embarrassed. I was wrong. The little lady showed me the back of her middle finger and said, "Fuck you." It had a nice emphatic tone to it.

I'd had enough of child rearing for the day so I stood, gathered my trash, and left her there polishing up for making a future husband's life unbearable.

Once again I had been reminded that when it comes to Catholic girls, Billy Joel didn't know what the fuck he was talking about.

The office door at the A-Aardvark limo service was locked. Nobody nowhere. I stepped over and peeked in a heavily tinted bay door window. The flash of a welder barely illuminated a guy in a welder's mask and cowboy boots. Charlie Boscoe had mentioned Elvis, but this guy was wearing clothes Tom Jones wouldn't mind being caught dead in.

I crossed in front of three tinted bay doors and went around the building. I had noticed a six-foot privacy fence as I came up from the other side and was hoping to break lucky. No luck; more fence. But not a good fence.

A yank or two gave me a foot to slide my skinny ass through. I nearly shit.

An antique rottweiler came out of his reverie, and I swear to God, he looked embarrassed to get caught asleep at the wheel. We read each other for a few seconds.

It seemed like my turn to say something. "What's up, dog?"

He didn't answer, he just got up stiffly, still looking a little embarrassed, and ambled over for a head scratch. I obliged. His grizzled nose went in my crotch and I figured he'd earned the liberty. I guess I passed the sniff test; he ambled back to his spot in the sun and plopped down.

A traffic door stood open at the back of the building and it seemed to be inviting me in. I took the invitation.

The welding was making popping sounds and casting a cobalt glow on several cars, none of which would pass for a limo. Hot? Sure. Limo? No.

A black Jag sedan was sitting among the suspects with trunk and hood both up. Grady was under the hood of a nice new Lexus, sparks flying around him.

I stepped over to the welder and flipped the switch labeled power. The sparks died; Grady cursed.

He uncurled, checked the rod against the underside of the hood and cursed again. The welding hood came up and showed me a face that could have been caught in a meteor shower at one time.

Grady wiggled the ground clamp and touched the rod to the car again. No dice; curse; toss the hood down; turn.

"Hi, Grady."

Judging from the way he jumped, it must have scared the shit out of him.

"Goddam. Who the fuck are you?"

I just kept smiling.

"We're closed here, buddy-ro."

I smiled on.

"How'd you get in here?"

"Same way the cars did." I did a Vanna White for him, showcasing the cars in case he'd missed them.

Grady was going shady on me. "Yeah? How's that?"

"Slipped in when nobody was looking."

Without taking his eyes off me, he laid the clamp with the welding rod in it on the car's fender. A hand went behind him, so I put one of mine on a hip, above my front pocket, close to where the Smith was hiding. My thumb slid under my shirt locating the grip.

Grady came out with a chrome comb and rearranged the grease on his head in a move he'd practiced a million times. The dent the welder's mask had made in the side of his head went away and the hair was perfect. Long, greasy, black and perfect. He held on to the comb. His eyes went down; they knew why my hand was where it was.

I'd say he was six-two or so, narrow shouldered, decent gut. A face you could race dirt bikes on, with a big hawk's beak. Eyes so full of nothing I should have been able to see the inside of his skull. Purple puff sleeved shirt; I couldn't put much of a guess on weight or condition. Dun-colored double knit, slash-pocket slacks belled unfashionably over fake-snake boots. Total package, Shady Grady the aardvark looked like he'd taken maybe two steps out of the primordial pool. One that landed in the late fifties, then one that landed smack dab in the early eighties. A fucking caveman. I could smell the inexpensive cologne across the room.

"Anybody says I steal cars is a fuckin' liar."

We showed each other our serious faces.

"Yeah?"

"Fuckin' A, yeah. Who tole you that shit?"

"Nobody said you *stole* cars." I broke first and grinned. His Adam's apple made me do it.

"Well, anybody says I do *anything* with hot cars is a fuckin' liar."

I was about to get a real show from the Adam's apple. "You know, Grady, you're a big, stupid-looking motherfucker but I got a hundred-dollar bill in my pocket says you won't call Charlie Boscoe and tell him he's a liar." Dramatic pause. "Wanna bet?"

I got a hundred bucks' worth of turkey necking. Grady went past shady over to cagey. "Yeah, I'll take that bet. Let's go in the office." He pointed with a finger that could have used some attention to hygiene.

"Tell you what, since I already had the drop on you once and it went so damn well, let's stick to that. You first." I laid out a cordial hand.

Grady hit the hairdo a few times, hid the comb. "Come on."

I followed the boot clomp across the garage and into the office. I didn't follow too closely.

A stocky Hispanic dude was sitting in the office wearing a tux shirt and black pants. It bumped me sideways a little because he wasn't there when I tried the front door and I didn't know where he came from. Fucking aardvarks were coming out of the woodwork now. I nodded and he mirrored the move and went back to his jack mag.

The office was a real place of business. Computers, calendars, the works. Decent piece of carpet.

Grady backed up to a desk and grabbed a phone, sliding it to him. "You got that hunnert in your pocket, slim?"

I grinned and showed him a grand, less what Charlie Boscoe had in his pocket. Chummed a bit; hid it.

His fingers did a dance on the phone face. From where I

was standing I could have heard the earpiece purr, could have heard Charlie's voice. I didn't hear shit. I stepped in on Grady a little.

Grady put his left leg on his right knee then his leg started itching, I guess. He scratched the pants leg up till I could see the fox at the top of the plastic boot. I stepped in again.

"Grady, you stick a hand in that boot, I'll knock you down so fucking fast your shadow won't know where you went." I threw in a big grin, no charge.

The Hispanic guy snickered back behind me. I don't know if it was that, the getting laughed at, or just that when your brain's not so big, you can't see yourself drawing into a losing hand. Grady went for the promised Colt. Bad move.

Jamming your hand down inside a sixteen-inch boot shaft when things are going to shit doesn't work. Ask Grady.

I bitch slapped him with my left to adjust his chin for a straight right with all I had from the shoulder. Lucky for Grady I was standing there to grab that left boot when he went ass backwards over the desk. Otherwise he might have hurt his head.

The free right foot kicked at me and I pulled the Smith with my unemployed left and stuck it in his crotch. Something behind me moved and I swung the gat around. My friendly Latin buddy went out the front door. I put the steel back in Grady's nuts. He settled down. Hanging by one leg didn't seem so bad now.

"The fuck you want, you crazy motherfucker?"

"I want that black Jag out there and I want the two crackers that jacked it."

"I got papers on that Jag."

"Right. Soon as the ink dries, you can take it out for a spin." I punched with the barrel. "The crackers, Grady."

31

"Fuck you." Damn bold talk from a man hanging upside down by one leg with a 9-millimeter in his business.

Grady's boot was in my right armpit, my arm under it. In a quick move, I hiked up on the leg. "Last chance to stay in the breeding pool, slick." I threw the thumb-latch safety and it sounded loud.

"You ain't gone just walk in here off the street and shoot nobody. Not in front o' no witness nohow."

"Uh-oh. Chico left, man." I lifted the pistol, dropped a cap, and it made a hole in the flap of double knit snagged up on my front sight. I would have seen more but I couldn't hold on to Grady.

He gave up the boot and the Colt fell out as he disappeared over the edge of the desk. I put my free hand on it as Grady's pompadour previewed the appearance of his face. The hair wasn't perfect anymore.

I rested my piece on Grady's nose when it appeared. "The crackers, Grady. And you got the wrong end up for the game we're playing here."

"Billy Joe Ratliff and Stiff Burry."

"Where could one find these industrious young men? Any given day?"

"Billy Joe lives on Sheeler Road in Apopka. At the big curve. Ugly yellow house trailer. I don't know where Stiff's livin' now. Maybe at Billy Joe's."

I nodded like he was a good boy. "You rekey the Jag?"

"Uh-huh."

"Where's the key?"

Grady's hand came up and pulled a drawer open. When he put his hand inside, I rapped his head with the gun barrel. "I'll handle it from here. You just sit on down and back up under the desk."

Grady disappeared and I could hear him moving around

down under there. I found a key that had a tag advising me it was for a *black Jaggar*. There was also a little fifty-dollar automatic there. I popped the clip out, stuck both in a back pocket.

The Colt had three pills. Two empties off the pin. Click, click, pull. Not a bad trick if you were in the habit of having guns taken off you. I shucked the three live ones out onto the carpet and yanked a cord out of a phone. I nabbed one of the waiting chairs from against the wall. I reached down and grabbed Grady's white plastic belt under the front of the desk's kick panel and pulled.

"Back up, how 'bout it?"

He was a good boy again and did as he was asked. I yanked hard, then looped the phone wire through the belt and tied it to the metal chair leg. It wouldn't keep him all day but I didn't give a shit where he spent the rest of the day. I needed maybe two minutes.

Grady's Colt in hand, I went back into the garage. I tossed the pistol in a drum filled with something green, maybe antifreeze. I added the little auto and its clip. A button with an arrow slid the bay door up and away.

I dropped the trunk and hood on the black Jag, stroked it till it purred, but I almost felt bad when I backed out. I wasn't sure Grady was smart enough to drop his pants. I didn't feel bad too long.

SEVEN

The cell phone on the nice leather seat next to me purred. I grabbed it, looked at the digits. A few gray cells clumped around them. Okay. The number Terry Sebring had traded for mine. I poked a key.

"I've missed you, Red."

Hesitation.

"Sloan? Is everything okay?"

I thought about it. "Far as I can tell. Why?"

"The scene on the Trail. What happened?"

"Just looking for some common language between me and the guys following you around."

More hesitation.

"Did you shoot them?"

"Not yet, but the future's always young."

"Oh, God." Relief. "I heard the shots and saw you standing there with a gun."

"Yeah. That's what I do for a living."

"Are you in trouble?"

"Not for that. It's the Trail, Terry. You've got to actually kill somebody to get any attention. Then you need to be inventive as to method to even make the B section." Reassurance: "We're still in business. You need your car?"

Terry wasted a few more cell seconds. "Did you find who took it?"

"I think so." One can never be sure.

"And you think you can get it back?"

"That much I'm sure of."

"Oh. So you know where it is?"

"Yeah." This was fun.

"Well?"

"Well what?"

"Where is it?"

"Right now it's going down Shady Lane. Wait." I took a left. "Now it's turning at the Kerouac house on Clouser." I was at the clapboard duplex where Kerouac supposedly jacked out *The Dharma Bums*. A monument to the wonders of whiskey, white crosses and butcher paper.

"You're following it?"

"I'm driving it. And it handles well."

We blew some more dough on dead air.

"I just left your house four hours ago."

I *wished* house. "So?"

"So this thing may be over sooner than we expected, then. Right?"

Heartbreak time. "No, Terry, it's not. The car was the easy part. Now I gotta go drag a couple of peckerwoods outta muck farm country, give 'em a chance to stay outta jail."

A nice sigh. "Oh, Sloan, this is so crazy."

She should be standing in Shady Grady's boot. "That's why I make the big bucks. You need the car?"

"No, not really."

"Good. I'll take it by a friend's, let him go over it. Get it re-rekeyed." Charlie Boscoe's. "It'll be safe there till you get ready for it."

"Thank you, Sloan. For the car, too. But thanks for helping me out."

"You thanked in advance. Ten thousand times. Keep your

head down, Red. I'll check in when there's something to talk about."

She was hesitant to let me go and I didn't get it. Maybe I was the channel marker she'd grabbed. Out past the breakers and drifting fast.

"Okay." Pause. "You want to come by this evening?"

Watch your step, Sloan. "Lemme have a little time on that, Red. You don't owe me. I'm still way out ahead of you."

Terry, the tough one, was back. "Whatever. Give me a call." And she was gone.

I drove along thinking about the deal Henry Flagler must've cut with the sun to get it to shine so bright. I thought about how Einstein must have laughed his ass off when he got credit for inventing relativity. I wondered why it didn't hurt as much to get a cavity filled as it used to.

I wondered why I didn't just stop the Jag and shoot myself in the fucking foot.

EIGHT

The sun had all but pulled its shift in that deal with Flagler and was headed west to party on the left coast. I was headed to Apopka. Same general direction as old dependable, but Terry's fancy Jag wasn't keeping up so good.

Apopka is the clump of lantana in the front yard. It's nice when it's in bloom, but when it's not, it just kind of looks like a weed. Muck farms and fern farms. Landfills and sandpits. Mexicans and rednecks. Yuppies and farmers. Indigenous as it was, you had to admire the fierceness with which Apopka maintained its own identity. Not an easy trick sitting smack dab in the shadow of the mighty money rat.

Sheeler Road peels off toward trailer park country about where Orlando gives the Trail back to Florida and it once again becomes highway 441, the Orange Blossom Trail. A half mile of fractured asphalt, Sheeler hooks ninety degrees right so as to be sure not to miss the dump on Keene Road. I assumed Grady had been talking this big curve.

A chalky drive that once had some gravel on it took me to a yellow-and-white mobile home. It didn't look like it had been mobile since about the Tet Offensive. There was lantana and palmetto in the yard. Beside the trailer a couple of azaleas had gone feral and tall; scraggly mutants enjoying the neglect.

I had to penalize Billy Joe Ratliff a few points for not having the required redwood deck. He had a set of shaky iron steps with a thirsty-looking red-nosed bulldog chained to it. Points back for the bulldog.

Pits scare me. They're about as noisy as a Mossad hit team and can be damn near as deadly. This guy just wanted some *agua*. He stood and stretched, shook good, rattling the piece of logging chain padlocked around his neck. He strained against the chain. If he had a tail, it would have been wagging. He didn't, so his ass was stuck with the job. The day was turning out to be a study in lackadaisical guard dogs.

There was a piece of garden hose on a PVC riser by the trailer. I spun the handle and let the water run fresh and cool. Fido looked at the wasted water, then at me like I was some demented god.

I still didn't trust him a hundred per, so I shot water in an arc over to a cut-down five-gallon pail. Fido didn't care if he took some to the head; his speckled tongue was hard put.

While he was occupied rehydrating I chanced moving in close enough to rap on the door. Bad move.

Fido came out of the pail so fast he slung water on me. I dropped the hose, maybe I threw it, and backpedaled faster than an election-year politico. Two more links in the chain, and I'd be five inches shorter in my right leg.

I yelled: *Hey!*-And the schizo fucker went down, then rolled over on his back. He may have been making nice, but one near collision with that set of chompers was plenty. I banged on the side of the trailer in a place the chain wouldn't reach. No response.

I took a peek in a window. The inside was about as charming as the exterior. Maybe only slightly dirtier, but no lantana growing in there yet. Beer bottles and a bag of reefer on a coffee table. Rolling papers. An ashtray big enough you needed a backhoe to empty it. Clothes on every other horizontal surface. No crackerjackers though.

There was movement. I cupped my hands and took another look. Nothing. Then two little heads peeked around a corner.

"Your dad home?" Through the window.

Heads gone. Heads back.

"Is your mom here?" As soon as I said it, I regretted it. I hoped they'd been taught to lie.

"She's at work." The voice was maybe six.

"My daddy's at Mimaw's gettin' drunk." That one was younger.

I mumbled "Jesus" at the ground. Then through the glass to the kids, "You got something to eat? You're not hungry, are you?" It was dinnertime in this zone.

A girl that fit the first voice stepped out and held up a big bag of chips. A smaller boy stepped out, showed me a bag of chocolate-coated Sweet Sixteen doughnuts and a chocolate-coated face.

It wasn't my business. I told myself it wasn't my business. They had their chip group and their doughnut group. What did I care?

"Bye, kids. Keep the door locked."

Two yessir's harmonized and I turned. The hose was still running so I topped off Fido's pail. He didn't care. I was old news and no fun.

Halfway to the car, I looked back. Two little faces were at the window. They looked like they wished I could stay and play.

Man, it's a fucked-up world. You gotta have a license to drive a car, but . . .

Enjoy dinner, babies.

NINE

First time I laid eyes on Raleigh Lightstep he was pointing a 10-millimeter Glock at my head. I don't hold it against him, because I was doing the same to him, slightly smaller caliber though. We had a felon in common at the time and stumbled across each other in some bushes outside this felon's mother's house. We had faced off for a few tense seconds. Then I found out Raleigh was a cop and I asked if I could lay my pistol on the ground. He said that would be a good idea. I did and we've been okay since. I guess.

At the time, Raleigh was on the sheriff's fugitive warrant squad, an elite, brass-nuts bunch of psychos who would have walked into hell to service a warrant on your ass. I'd rather have stuck my hand in a bucket of rabid rats than do what those guys did. Picking up losers already run ragged. Guys who'd made the decision, most of them armed.

That wasn't enough for Raleigh. When Orange County decided to build a drug squad, Raleigh couldn't wait. He made a hell of a storm trooper, too. Until one night, in a case of itchy trigger finger, Raleigh got knee-popped by one of his own.

Now he worked in Central Booking at the county hotel on Thirty-third Street. Sitting on all that bad-ass all day, taking it out on his friends. I wouldn't say it to his face though. Not the part about being his friend. Raleigh would accuse me of being presumptuous.

I had gone by Charlie Boscoe's on the way home, grabbed Shiny and got him to drop me at the Dairy King to get my junk. No Catholic girls, no aardvarks in sight. I headed cribward to call Raleigh, say shit to him I wouldn't say standing in front of his large ass.

As I was working, I figured I should check in with my electronic secretary. *Nada* but a guy telling me, and being damned professional and sincere, how I could consolidate bills *and* lower my mortgage. I rent a three-room apartment that was once a garage, you fuckhead. My mortgage got any lower, I'd live in a cardboard box.

Since my mortgage rates were fine, I erased the plea and buzzed Raleigh.

"Thirty-third Street Jail. Lightstep."

"Whasup, my dog?" I put a lot on the *dog* part.

Raleigh was searching around for some shit he'd been saving for a special occasion. I knew him well enough to know it was going to be ugly.

"Fuck, Sloan, you *wish* you was black."

What do you say to something like that? How do you respond to a 250-pound racist black man who could, and would, pick you up and, without putting the gimp leg to any trouble, toss you across the room like a Velcroed midget? I said: "And what does Raleigh Lightstep wish he was?"

"He wish he was talkin' to somebody else 'sides you."

"Yeah? Why's he wish that?"

"Cause you 'bout to ask me for somethin' and I'm gone tell you 'bout my needs and you gone whine and waste my time. But you know what?"

"I'm gonna give it to you anyway."

"Mmm-hmm. Why you do it, then? Take up my time like that?"

"It's the only relationship we got, sweetie. If it wasn't for that, you wouldn't spend any time with me."

"Shut up, Sloan. The fuck you want?"

"Apopka boys. Billy Joe Ratliff and Stiff Burry. And anything you got on the top of your head about Shady Grady Somebody at Aardvark Limo."

There was a sound I didn't recognize. "Excuse me. Was that a laugh?"

It was. Raleigh fucking Lightstep, who tossed smiles around like they were 747s, was laughing. Yeah, it was low and wicked, Barry-White-on-opium stuff, but it was a laugh.

"What's so fucking funny?"

"You done took to chasin' lost cars." More laugh. "Whatcha gone be doin' next? Jumpin' outta closets with a camera? Gettin' cats outta trees?" More of the unpleasant laugh.

"Goddam, Raleigh, you been in the evidence locker again?"

"Damn, Sloan. That's the hardest I laughed since Harvey Dennis shit his pants the time that Russian shot 'im."

"Making memories right and left, aren't we? I take it you know where I could find these boys?"

"Mmm-hmm. They stay with us from time to time. The first two, anyway. I know Grady from the DUKE boy days." The sheriff's fascist drug squad.

"He moving product?" I didn't read Grady as a trader.

"Nah. Ended up with a car had a dead Dominican's cocaine in it. We sat on Grady and wired his ass, got him to go talk to the Rickies who was lookin' for the dust."

"Sounds too easy."

"Mmm-hmm. Grady so fuckin' nervous he blow up about fifteen seconds inside, start yellin' in his lapel for help. We had to run in to keep the motherfuckers from killin' 'im."

Why? "He didn't look that steady to me either. You got any ideas on where to find Ratliff or Burry?"

"Gimme five; call back." He was gone.

I gave him fifteen.

"Lightstep."

"Make me happy."

"Mmm-mmm. You ruint."

"You gonna hurt me?"

"Man, I'm gone beat you like a rent-to-own wife."

"You got them on a platter for me?"

"One of 'em."

Shit. "Which arm you want to go with that leg?"

"Hey, you one to be talkin', motherfucker. You all about chargin' the big rate. Want people to respect your skill. Same thing on this end, dog. It ain't like I'm askin' for a percentage on what you done put in your pocket. And I know what you get. Nah, Sloan, all I want is a nice relaxin' evenin' with a friend. Good conversation, shit like that."

"I'll have to get a new outfit."

"Fuck you. I ain't talkin' 'bout your skinny drawed-up cracker ass. I got a lady friend needin' to be impressed. At a nice place. Bottle o' good wine. Candles."

"Goddam, Raleigh, you gonna start reciting poetry here? What? You in love or something?"

"Love? What's that shit? Love?"

"I see. You still doing Chinese?"

"Oh, dog, you ain't gettin' off that easy."

I winced. Yeah, it wasn't my money, but like I say, it's all me and Raleigh got. "French?"

"Chef Henry's." Eastern European, whatever the fuck that is.

"How much is this setting me back?"

"Shit, I don't care. Just call in a credit card number for Saturday, party of two, 'bout eight."

"Fuck you."

"Oh shit, Sloan, I gotta go. My desk is piled up with all kinda shit needs to get done. Sorry 'bout your luck. Maybe, you call back when I ain't so busy, we could cut a deal you could live with. See you, dog."

"Son of a bitch. Two hundred bucks, Raleigh. That's it. Tops."

"Hey, I'll bring my calculator. Whatchu tippin' these days? Twenty points?"

"A buck a person."

"Mmm-hmm. Greasy spoon shit you eat at, they prob'ly wipe your table twice, money like that. I'll do a solid fifteen, make you feel good 'bout yourself."

"Where's my boy?"

"Sittin' 'bout ten feet behind me givin' Fat Tommy the bail bondsman all his worldly possessions. Look like he gone get to spend the night at home. I knew you an' me could deal, so I greased the wheels of justice for you, had 'im brought on down."

"He in for jacking?"

"Nah. Ain't nothin' that serious. This time. D and D. He look like he got drunk and talked somebody into whippin' his ass."

"You think you could misplace his paper for twenty, thirty minutes? Give me time to catch him in your parking lot?"

"Hmm. Lemme see."

"Jesus Christ, man. I can't do anything else for you but come over and do breakfast in bed for you and the lady."

"That ain't bad. What you consider your A.M. specialty?"

"Fuck it. Deal's off. If I can't catch him tonight, I'll run him down on my own."

"You serious?"

"No. I'd cook the fucking eggs but I'd be so pissed off you'd be crazy to eat 'em."

"Well, ain't no free rides. Couple of brandies and extra desserts."

"That Louis the Fourteenth shit or whatever it is you drink when you're trying to impress?"

"But of course." There was a little French accent attempt on that part. Raleigh might want to reconsider the maintenance dosage on his chill pills. "Only the best for Sloan's friends."

"See you in a half hour."

"Don't come your ass in here. You crazy? Stiff Burry a husky dude with blond hair stick straight up." A chair squeaked. "He wearin' a red shirt say something 'bout America."

"It probably says: Only in America could you find somebody stupid enough to toss down three hundred bucks on a two-bit horse thief. Bye."

TEN

Easy. That's all I was looking for. There's only so much holding people upside down and shaking them a man can do in a day and stay on point. I was hoping a blend of threat and dough would loosen Stiff Burry up, give us both the warm-and-fuzzies.

Maybe eight miles and it took most of a half hour to do John Young Parkway. I caught every fucking light toward the jail. Then there it was. Jail World.

A jail at night is a spectacular sight. Something dripping right out of Coppala's brain. Sparkles dancing on the concertina like wicked little fairies playing in too much sodium light. A freaky yellow-pink glow. Miles of concrete and chain link. The windows in the guard stacks are tinted dark enough, but you know they're in there. You know they'll shoot.

The whole message is: *Try it, sucker.* What's more surprising than the number of chumps that do try it is the number of chumps that make it. Enough smarts to get out of a locked steel box, jump a razor-coated compound under enough light to grow sinsemilla. Then get caught walking down the side of the road in jail pajamas, eating HoHos and chain-smoking Camels. All the guys lined up to try it, looks like recidivism would pay better.

I knew which door they turned you loose at. I'd used it a couple of times. The best spots in the lot were labeled: Orange County Employees Only. I backed into one and shut down everything but the college radio station. Some post-punks

46

were either cacophoning or tuning up, I couldn't tell. I *could* tell they were about three chords short of a garage band. I punched a button and got a guy named Drew jerking some jerk around on the talk station. I punched another and let Eddie Vedder bore me until a stocky guy in a red shirt used my door.

The red shirt stopped, did the just-got-outta-jail deep-breathing thing, capped it with the required check to make sure the sky's still there. Yep, still there.

How you doing, Stiff?

I'd have called the hair gold. It could have been spray painted, it was that gold. He assessed the parking lot, maybe thinking about a loaner, thought better and hiked out for the gate.

He was an American. Grade A, according to the shirt. The cuffs of his droopies were shredded and dirty. The closer he got to the gate, the better his nerve was getting. They come out the door with yessir all over their faces and hit the gate with fuck-the-cops taking its place. Stiff threw a little whigger in his walk, rounded the gatepost, threw a middle finger at the pokey. The pokey didn't care.

He walked north after he cleared the property, halfheartedly sticking a thumb in the direction of home. John Young, McCleod and the I-4 collide by the jail. So do four or five commuters every day. An intersection from hell that Stiff knew no one in their right mind would stop in. He kept kicking it.

Good timing put me north on John Young, just past malfunction junction, as Stiff Burry put out a sincere thumb. I pulled right.

He got in smiling like he'd been in jail. His face was scuffed and he wouldn't be doing much babe winking for a day or two out of his right eye.

"Where you headed, my man?" I was friendly. I was a regular guy.

"Apoka," using the correct indigenous pronunciation, dropping the second *p* in Apopka.

"Your lucky night."

"Where you headed?"

"Mount Dora."

"Cool."

I looked at him. "Maybe it's not your lucky night. That eye hurt?"

"Some. Fuckin' slimeball bouncer at Cactus Club. Fucker sucker-punched my ass."

I bet. I bet Stiff was so drunk, the guy could have sent the punch ground mail and Stiff wouldn't have seen it coming. "Fucking bouncers." I was on his side. I was a commiserating son of a bitch.

"Nice car."

"Thanks." It wasn't.

"Seventy-four?"

"Seventy-six."

"Yeah. This body's the best one."

This style was the cheap one. "Listen, I got a hundred-dollar bill in my pocket I wanna give you. I saw you come outta Thirty-third Street and know the bondsman got everything you had but a promissory note on your asshole. You want the hundred?"

Stiff looked at me, nervous. "Just cause I spend the night in jail once in a while don't mean I go that way."

I was grinning. "What way's that?" I knew what way. Maybe I was having a little fun.

"You know." He didn't want to insult me, I guess. "That way. None o' that funny stuff."

"No funny stuff, huh? Matter of fact, I wanna help you out

there. Help you preserve your rosy virginity by keeping your worthless ass outta Florida State Prison up at Starke. You interested, Stiff?"

Hard as he looked, he couldn't place me. I helped him. "You don't know me. We've got a common interest in a black Jag you and Billy Joe Ratliff found in front of a strip mall."

There were a lot of ups and downs, but I think Stiff was more comfortable with the Jag than when he thought I was hitting on him.

"Don't know nothin' about that."

"You need to think about the hundred-dollar bill, then. If the trip to Starke doesn't bother you."

He started to speak and I interrupted. "Think about it, Stiff. You think I didn't have proof you took the Jag, you'd be sitting there? I gotcha cold, my man."

We finally put the brain to work. "The fuck are you?"

"A friend of the lady's."

More cerebrating.

"I know where it is."

"No you don't." I could feel him looking over. "I'll tell you though. It's at Charlie Boscoe's." I let that sink in. "Wanna go steal it again?"

"No." I was a friend of Charlie Boscoe's; he didn't even want to look at me.

"I didn't think so. One question, a hundred bucks. There was a little deal they call a Palm Pilot in that car. Here's the money question: Who ended up with that dingus?"

The light at Colonial caught us and I looked over. Confusion. Stiff didn't think it would be that easy.

"That's all you want? Who got the computer thing?"

"A hundred bucks' worth I want it."

"Shit." He looked over, grinning, relieved. "And I thought you was some queer or somethin'. Grady Pelham. Does

mechanic work at a limo place. Aardvark's or something like
that."

Ah fuck. I should have shook Grady harder while I had
him upside down. I never figured him for being that smart.
"He know what it was?"

"Yeah. Grady ain't bad with shit like that, computers and
stuff." He hesitated. "You know the woman's a whore?"

"Yeah. How did you guys find out?"

"Grady found a list with, like, nicknames and phone
numbers. Another place, it had big hotels like Hilton and
Peabody and shit. It had five hundred or seven hundred or
eight hundred beside it."

"Yeah? So Grady figured it from there?"

"Uh-huh. Listen. You think she gets that much for a piece
o' ass?"

"No. I think that's what she gets per hour."

"Goddam, brother. There ain't a fuckin' pussy in the world
worth that kinda scratch. Is there?"

"I don't know, Stiff. I never tried it."

He looked at me like I was trying to sell him a handful of
rat shit. "You ain't never tried pussy or you ain't never tried
that one?"

My face was smiling. "That one."

"You said you was friends. Why not?"

"I don't have five hundred bucks spare."

"She don't do no freebies? Not even for friends?"

I pulled off the road. "Would you? You could get that kinda
payola? You ready to get out, Stiff?"

I let Stiff Burry and his C-note ride the thumb on north and
I doubled around to my hutch.

I made a glass of chocolate milk, stop the Coneys I'd had
earlier from barking all night. Poured a Newcastle on top of

it. The daybed looked good, so I rounded up all the pillows in the joint and propped myself up and put on *The Daily Show*. Stewart was funny enough but I'd seen the report before. I drifted around, bumped my head on a few stray thoughts: what I knew, what I thought, what I didn't know.

Right before the Sandman tracked me down and banged my head against the moon, I remembered thinking that this shit was going way too fucking easy. I should have held that thought.

ELEVEN

There was enough cop power at A-Aardvark Limo to quell a Seattle free-trade rebellion. Yellow tape. Guys with gadgets and gizmos. A meat wagon.

The bay doors were all up, and the Hispanic guy from yesterday and a guy with hair like Dilbert's boss's were getting double- and triple-teamed off to one side. I pulled in the parking lot across the street at Saint Charles Borromeo and waited for Grady to show.

I didn't wait long. Two guys in light blue shirts rolled him out in a bag. The length of the bag strongly supported my suspicion, but the pointy toes sticking up confirmed it: Dead Grady.

I had problems. Terry had problems. Grady Pelham had some problems yesterday, but not this morning.

I pulled out and headed north, no idea where I was going. Just ride for a bit. Ride it out.

About Bear Lake, I caught my finger caressing my piece, clicking the nail back and forth on the checkered grip. I didn't catch myself coming up with any bright ideas, though.

Edgewater dumped me on a street called Rose. But what's in a name? It had two more before it dumped me on Altamonte. I headed west.

Full circle, I ended up back at the part right after Grady. I cut back again and caught Billy Joe's road and found his unmobile home where I'd left it.

A beat-up eighties-model Camaro was near the iron stair. The passenger door was open. A rice rocket was leaning against the trailer by Fido.

Fido's stump was wagging, but I knew something about his fickle disposition; it made me think about where the chain ended.

I knocked on the side of the trailer; Fido came out of the hole; the chain jerked; the bike went down. A hairy face appeared at the window near me. I smiled for it. It scowled.

Directly, the door jerked open. Either the place was on fire or someone had figured out what the reefer and rolling papers were for. I picked the latter.

"What?" A stupid grunt.

The guy with the grunt also had a fine brown beard and a mullet hairdo. Skinned on the sides down to the white walls, long hank at the back. Even had the flattop part. He looked like a fucking nincompoop. Tank top. Baggy, sloppy-assed shorts. Pricey hightops, laces gone and the tongues wagging at me. A short, fat, hairy motherfucker from all I was seeing.

"You must be Billy Joe."

He squinted some for me, shook the hair to make sure I'd noticed it.

"Who says?"

"I gave Stiff a ride part of the way home last night."

He relaxed, nearly smiled. "The gentleman with the hundred-dollar bills."

I nodded some. "Where's Stiff?"

His hairdo jerked. "In here. You need to see 'im?"

"Need to see both of you, Billy Joe. I've got some exciting news for ya'll."

"Yeah? What's that?"

I pointed to the dog. "He okay?"

Billy Joe looked at the mangy red-nose. "Fuckin' pussy. You

yell, he lays on his back for an hour. Come on in." To the dog, loud: "Sit down, Mutt!"

Mutt hit his back and I hit the steps. Stiff Burry and another guy, a kid with hormones exploding through his complexion, sat at a round table under a wagon-wheel chandelier. It would have been brighter if more than one lonely bulb was working.

Stiff looked up, turned and exhaled a lungful. "Hey, Corvette man. How you doin'? Come on. I picked up some krypy with the bill you put on me." A Plexiglas bong smoldered out wisps of proof. The pimply kid nabbed the bong, made himself cough pretty bad and poked it at me. I declined and he sat the bong on the table like he might be balancing an arrow on its sharp end.

"What's your name, my man?"

The kid looked up, stoned stupid. "Me?"

Stiff laughed. "You fucked up, Gerald?"

The kid swung around to Stiff. "Huh?"

Billy Joe came around and sat, then he and Stiff giggled at Gerald some.

"Look at me, Gerald." He did. "You aren't driving that crotch rocket out there, are you?" I wasn't getting much from Gerald's face.

Stiff took his turn. "Fuck no. That's mine. He's one 'o the boys in the hood."

"Get rid of him."

Billy Joe and Stiff looked at me. Billy Joe went south. "Excuse me?" Had a real man-of-the-house tone to it.

"Listen. I know it's your house, but we got serious business." They weren't believing me. "Grady just left the limo service in an ambulance."

"Yeah? Why do we care?"

Gerald got sincere. "Why do you care, Billy Joe?"

Billy Joe: "Shut up, Gerald."

All eyes on me. "They didn't use the lights and sirens when they left. Know why?" Then to Gerald: "Know why, Gerald?"

Gerald: "Uh-uh. Why?"

Billy Joe took his eyes out of mine and rose. He came around and grabbed Gerald's arm. "Come on. You need to leave."

Gerald wasn't following this any better than the other parts. A lot of sounds beginning with "wh" kept coming out of his mouth. They stopped when Billy Joe closed the door on him. I took Gerald's seat and was glad to have my head down below the line of smoke in the room.

Billy Joe was pretty straight by the time he came back. He sat, trying to toad himself out, making up for height deficit and being out of his game. "Now." His arms bowed around and rested on the table. "What's this shit about Grady?"

"Grady was rolled outta the garage about an hour ago in a plastic bag." A good, solid hit.

Stiff: "Say what?" Over the shortstop's head.

Billy Joe: "No shit?" And between the left fielder's legs.

"No shit. Grady's down." I cakewalked across home plate.

Billy Joe made it sound cheeky, but he really wanted to know. "What's that got to do with us?"

I showed them one of my good smiles. "If somebody put a gun to your head, wouldn't you give 'em Grady and Stiff?"

"Not Stiff." Fists bumped on that one.

"Bullshit. Stiff sold Grady for a hundred bucks. I held Grady by the ankles and he gave me both of you free of charge. The fuck you think you're fooling? What you need to do is shut the hell up and listen. I'll see if I can figure out a way to keep your sorry asses out of the bag."

"Why would the guy 'at killed Grady wanna find us?" Stiff was coming down from the sinsemilla.

"Fuck if I know. Maybe he's not looking for you. Maybe

I'm just being silly." I made the point with some deadpan. "You feeling lucky? Either one of you?"

Billy Joe got up and came back with four Buds in a six-pack carton. He grabbed one, decapped it and hid some. Stiff reached one. Another gulp and Billy Joe said, "Talk. We're listening."

"Follow me here, boys. You took the Jag. There was an electronic thing in it called a Palm Pilot. There were some names and phone numbers on it. Grady started making calls. Now he's dead. These guys may or may not be swimming upstream. They are? You two, me, and the lady, we all got problems."

We chewed that. Billy Joe wanted to know why I thought they had our names again.

"They don't have mine. But they know I'm connected to the Jag and the lady. They know I'm looking for you two. Unless you think Grady committed suicide because his conscience was bothering him."

Billy Joe was doing the talking. "So what're we supposed to do about it?"

"You tell me everything you know and go get your asses in a hole somewhere. And take your kids."

"Where the hell we goin'? We ain't got no money." Billy Joe knew I had some.

"You tell me something I don't know, I'll back you on a camping trip. You got a tent?"

"Yeah." He looked me over good. "Where you wanna start? Takin' the car?"

"No. No. Let's go to you handing Grady the Palm Pilot."

"Awright. We didn't even know what the fuckin' thing was. It looked like it was worth a few bucks. We bring Grady the car, show him the doohickey. He's fuckin' with it. Punching

56

buttons. It makes a little tune and Grady says he's inside or something."

Stiff chimed in. "He said, 'I'm in'. Like in that movie."

Billy Joe looked irritated. "Anyway, he punches numbers and then goes, 'Lookit here. I believe this woman's a whore'."

"Nah. He said, 'Lookit. The woman's a hooker'."

"Whatever." Billy Joe didn't give much of a damn about a rose with another name either.

"How'd Grady figure that?"

"Grady goes: 'Same name, same hotel, same time, same day every month.' Grady could be pretty savvy sometimes."

So can a cockroach.

"So when did Shady Grady decide to start calling people?"

Billy Joe shrugged. "I don't know. He asked us what she looked like, and what he did was he went to some o' them hotels at the times was in the gizmo. He seen her meetin' dudes an' then goin' upstairs an' stuff." There goes Terry's theory about it being hard to find her.

"So now he's sure she's a hooker, he starts calling people on the list. That how it went?"

"Uh-huh. He said he'd made a couple of calls but hadn't seen no money yet."

"You know if he was working with anybody else on this thing?"

Billy Joe eyed me. "You seem to know a helluva lot about all this shit. Maybe it was you done Grady."

"Yeah, Einstein, I talked Grady to death and now I came here to do the same thing to you and Stiff. Get real."

Billy Joe finished the Bud, got him another, took a good slug off it. "Yeah. They was somebody else. We was back in there a couple of days later an' Grady said we wouldn't believe it. He'd jackpotted. He called one o' the numbers and the guy told him he was dabbling in chickenshit. Maybe they need to hook up. Show Grady to get the big numbers."

"That when they started taking pictures?"

Billy Joe: "Yeah. Grady said the man had a long distance camera."

"Nah it wasn't. It was some kinda something about lenses." Stiff.

"It don't make no fuckin' difference what it's called, asshole. It's a goddam long distance camera. Shit." Pull from the beer bottle.

"So Grady and this guy from the list, they do any good?"

"I'on't know. We never heard no more. Ain't seen Grady in a few days now."

Stiff shook his head. "Looks like Grady found somebody he didn't wanna find."

We agreed around the table. "Anyone else? Anything at all?" The way they looked at each other, I knew there was something else. "Come on guys, help me out here. I'm the only one sticking around to make this go away."

Billy Joe reared back, finished the beer, said, "One more time, hoss, exactly who the hell are you now?"

"Like I told Stiff last night, the lady's a friend of mine. I take care of problems for friends of mine sometimes. Sometimes nobody tells me what I need to know and I just fuck things up worse." I slid my wallet out and found them a couple of my CRISIS ABATEMENT cards with my cell phone number on it. Somebody else's name, but my number.

"You think of anything, call. That is, if I don't fuck up and we all go to jail." I had a smile so nice it would have pried an orange from between Anita Bryant's knees.

Billy Joe gripped the edge of the table as he tipped back in his chair, breathed deep. He looked over at still semi-stupid Stiff. "Give it to 'im."

Stiff wiggled his ass loose from the chair and dug in a hip pocket that was actually down about mid thigh. A dingy triple-folded piece of printer paper hit the table on a spot where there wasn't a bottle or a dish or an ashtray. He missed the bong too.

It unfolded to be a list. I brushed the sand out of the creases and read.

A few I knew: *Chien, Oie, Lapin,* and, of course, *Escargot.* Must have been one of her favorites: the snail. The rest escaped me.

Across the page from each was a ten-digit phone number. I knew they were phone numbers because I recognized some area codes. Some I didn't.

"Where'd you get this?"

The boys traded smiles like they'd lifted the Hope Diamond. "Grady's desk," Billy Joe told me; Stiff added to the suspense: "With his ass standin' right there, too."

"How'd you know what it was?"

Billy Joe again. "I seen it that day on the—what'd you call that Palm thing? Palm Pilot?" I nodded him on. "He showed us when he found it. Them funny words. What is that shit? Some kinda code or somethin'?"

"Yeah. Was Grady doing the calling?" I would have been surprised.

"Nah. He said he was keepin' a copy in case the man fucked him. Said that was his ticket."

"It was his ticket, all right. You two don't have any idea who this new man was?"

Dual head wags. Billy Joe said, "I'on't think Grady even knew the dude's name. Somethin' he said. Somethin' 'bout maybe followin' him. What'd he say, Stiff?"

Stiff thought about it for long enough. "Somethin' about

59

insurance. Yeah. If he could find out who the guy really was, he'd see he didn't get fucked. Must not a trusted the man."

Well hell, there goes honor among thieves. Pretty soon I won't believe in anything. "Last question. Was Grady scared of the man? You dig what I'm saying?"

That one required some silent consultation. The dual head wags again.

Billy Joe: "If you mean like killin' him or somethin', nah. Grady laughed about what a dink the guy was. Grady was more scared the guy would go south on him. Said the guy's business was goin' to shit and it made Grady nervous. What'd he call 'im, Stiff?"

"The Brain."

Nobody knew why Grady called him the Brain. Billy Joe wanted to know: "You think the man killed Grady?"

The answer was real obvious to me, but I hadn't been puffing kryptonite all morning either. "If I was a cop, he'd be the guy I was looking for. There's a couple of other guys around too. A couple of cowboy hats in a Lincoln."

Billy Joe wanted to know who they were.

I shrugged for him. "Got me."

I refolded the sheet and pocketed it, retrieved some green, and dealt out two hundred apiece. "Go right now. Get your wife and kids," to Billy Joe. Then to both, "And get your asses outta town. You gotta a cell number?"

Billy Joe: "Yeah. My wife does." He gave me the number with some advice. "Make sure you talk to me, not the bitch."

"Sure, Billy Joe." I stood, leaned on the table with my knuckles and gave Billy Joe some advice. "By the way, I ever come by here again and that dog's outta water, or I see those two kids here alone eating dinner outta plastic bags, I'll call SPCA first, then county services. And if I'm still as pissed as I was yesterday when I left here, I'm gonna come by your mama's house and kick your drunk redneck ass. You get all that down?"

He heard me but he didn't say anything about it. I yelled at the dog as I cleared the door. Fido fell over, feet kicking air. When I looked up, a sad little car, a disposable station wagon, yellow to match the trailer, was dragging a chalky plume up the drive. It dragged the plume into the yard and stopped. Two little heads popped out open windows. I'd seen them before.

Chocolate-face said, from the window, "Hey, mister. I know you."

The little girl was back inside the car, facing a young woman of twenty or so. They spoke while looking at me occasionally. It didn't look so good.

Most of the boy was hanging out the window and he tumbled out, sliding headfirst down the side of the car. The woman yelled "Willie" and made a late grab. Willie hit the ground running. He stopped in front of me and mimicked my stance, arms folded, legs a little apart. He squinted up at me. "My daddy's home now."

"Yeah, I know, partner. I saw him."

"How you doing?" This to the woman who walked up. The little girl peered around her leg.

The woman, really a girl, had on a loose violet top, cotton, and jean shorts that couldn't have been any shorter. Barefoot, but not pregnant. Dishwater blonde hair in ponytails. She was almost bony and maybe even a little gawkish, but somehow pretty. Maybe beauty to come. She'd have been prettier if she had smiled.

"Come here, Willie." Then to me, "You the one watered the dog yesterday?"

"Yeah."

"'Preciate it. I was late to work and I just forgot." She looked down, embarrassed. "An' I don't leave my kids on their own. Somethin' happened yesterday and Billy Joe had to go to his mama's, then somethin' happened over there and he got stuck at her house."

Yeah. How about he got his lips stuck around the neck of a Budweiser bottle? "I heard. Don't worry about it."

She smiled and was pretty. So damn young.

"You get to see Billy Joe?"

"Yeah. We got to talk a little bit."

She looked off at the trailer, the smile evaporating into something more dismal. "It was nice of you to water the dog and all, but I wish ya'll wouldn't do no tradin' at the house. I've asked Billy Joe over and over, but. . . . "

"I'm not in the trading business, sweetheart. I brought bad news. I guess I'm in the bad news business."

She nodded, studied me. "Well, see you sometime."

"Hey." I brought her back around. "What's your name?"

I got the smile again. "Rachel."

"And what's little bit's name? Behind you there?"

"That's Tammie."

"Hey, Tammie." I got a very small "Hey" back for it.

"My name's Willie Joe Ratliff Junior."

"I thought your name was trouble."

"My name ain't trouble. You a dumb-ass or somethin'?"

"Willie Joe Ratliff, you watch your mouth."

I said, "I asked for it," while Willie pulled out on his lips, watching his mouth.

I looked down and saw my right hand peeling off a couple of bills. "Here." I peeled another, held them out there.

Rachel wouldn't take them. "What's that for?"

"I don't know, maybe I gotta crystal ball, Rachel. It tells me you folks are gonna be taking a little vacation soon. Maybe

Saint Augustine or somewhere. Buy you and the kids some vacation duds. You got vacation duds?"

She took the money but looked at it like it might vaporize at any second. "Thanks, but I don't understand. We ain't goin' nowhere."

"You never know, Rachel. One day you might just surprise yourself, fool right around and go somewhere. Have fun."

TWELVE

When I walked in on two cowboy hats back at my place, the moment became electric.

I went red-hot and pulled fast. The cowboy I could see smiled from under the brim, hands coming up innocent, a big, shiny government-issue .45 curled up on his lap. The other hat, seated back to me, turned enough for me to see a grin. Just hanging around Sloan's crib smiling up a storm.

Unless double knit had sneaked back in while I was staying out of malls, these boys were as out of vogue as cold Grady. What bothered me more than the polyester prayer-meeting outfits was the grins. The grins weren't bad. The grins were talking to me.

"See 'im, Ray Gene? Son bitch pulls like he means business."

Ray Gene agreed and thought I pulled fast too. He drawled about it a little.

What I had was two red-dirt Alabama boys. The best news was, I wasn't lying in the front yard with a .22 slug in the back of the head.

The smiles were telling me all about it. They were saying they could have had me eight ways by now. Might even take me now if I wasn't fast and sure. We didn't try me; we just grinned some while I moved across and got ringside. We grinned some more.

The one who initially spoke dipped his hat, said, "Evenin', Mr. Sloan. I'm Cecil. This here's Ray Gene."

Ray Gene showed me a hat dip, called me sir, even if they both had fifteen, twenty years on me. A twin to Cecil's .45 was relaxing in Ray Gene's hand, lying across a thigh.

Cecil asked, "You do know why we're here, don't you, son?"

"I could guess."

Cecil smiled out some good-old-boy. "See, Ray Gene. I tole you he was gonna be a pisser. After that shit with that Lincoln rent-a-car."

"How'd that work out for you?"

Ray Gene had a shrug that said he didn't give much of a shit. "We just tole 'em we takened a wrong turn and ended up in the quarters. Said one o' the boys down there took a pop at us and we had to run for it."

"They buy it?"

"I guess enough. They give us a ride down to the competition."

That was about all we had in common; the small talk went flat.

They were interesting but the gat in my hand was getting heavy. "I back off, the woman gets to walk away too?"

Ray Gene lifted his hat and mopped a pale scalp with a nylon handkerchief. "An' see, Cecil. I tole you he was smarter'n he looks."

I didn't think it was that smart. I was alive equaled they wanted to trade. I didn't have much to trade.

"The woman's the deal, guys. She walks, I walk."

Cecil shrugged out, "She ain't part o' our arrangement. Our man was hoping you'd understand. Go talk to 'er for us. You do that?"

I nodded. "Yeah. I'll tell her where we're at. You planning on taking those envelopes?"

The envelopes Terry had given me, the one with the title

and the list, the other with the photos, were lying in front of Cecil. That wasn't were I'd left them.

Cecil: "Uh-huh. An' ask the little lady don't be printin' no more of these, awright?"

"Sure. What if I say you're not taking them?"

Cecil's hand floated to the automatic. "Then me an' you an' Ray Gene got a problem."

We all grinned over that; different grin though. A tad tighter.

Cecil asked; "We got a problem?"

I gave it some thought. "No. Your business in Orlando done now?"

Cecil looked at Ray Gene. "Not bad till he went nosy on us, huh, Ray Gene?"

The Dixie Mob stood and grinned. I guess we'd had a good old time. Cecil got his envelopes. When he had the knob in his hand, he turned, looking around Ray Gene's hat.

"We left your money in your underwear drawer. Put another five in there the man wanted you to have." He put a pair of cold blue eyes on me. "You know what I tole him when he said give it to you?"

"You told him you'd do me for half that."

Cecil laughed, said, "Come on, Ray Gene. This boy's too damned fast for us old dogs. You ain't bad, son, but you oughta work on that nosy part."

The door or something in that direction held my attention for a while after they drifted. When I got up to get a beer, I realized I still had a gun in my hand.

I sat it on a table and wiped my sweaty hands on my pants. I felt like I'd been caught on the trestle, lain down and the train passed over me. I needed that beer.

The Newcastle comforted the near-death jits enough I found Terry's cell number. I fed it to my phone and waited.

"Hi."

"Hey, sweetheart. Which side of town are you on?"

"Do we need to meet?"

"Yeah."

"North. And I'm free."

The male mind makes something out of everything. "Meet me at the rest area between Sanford and Lake Mary. Which side?"

She thought. "Either."

"Eastbound. See you in thirty minutes."

"Sloan?"

"Yeah?"

"What's up. You sound different."

"Do I?" Maybe because I just stepped in front of a train and I don't know why I'm still alive. "See you in thirty minutes. Westbound."

"You said eastbound."

"Just checking you." Sure I was.

THIRTEEN

About the time Terry showed, I had figured out what it meant to be alive. More accurately, why I wasn't dead. I might mention my notions to her.

She found my car and slid hers in beside it. I got out and went around to the passenger side. It was warm enough, even in the shade. She kept the AC cranked.

"What's up, Red?"

"Hi, Sloan. Bad news?" I looked at her face. How bad would news have to be to be bad news to Terry Sebring?

I shrugged. "There is definitely a client involved. The guy who sold him the gizmo got dead." I slowed down.

She looked away, looking out the front window at nothing, nothing on her face. "Well. It's started."

"What's started?"

"I'm a Sebring. This is what happens."

"Before you start feeling like the victim of some random curse, let me tell you, somebody deliberately hired two Dixie Mob boys not to kill me and you. Seems their team just wants everyone to forget it; go home."

She had exactly nothing to add. I took her turn.

"Paid me another five not to get killed. Oh, and to talk to you. Tell you the situation."

"The way you're looking at me, that should mean something. I'm sorry; it doesn't."

"I guess that's not exactly *Jeopardy!*-category stuff. The Dixie works outta Phoenix City, Alabama. Across the line from Fort Benning in Georgia. They've had good luck with army bases. From there, they spread out across the south. Not this far south usually.

"Unlike most"—clubs? companies?—"organizations like that, they don't use the young red-hots in the fold for men's work. Girls, slots, numbers, whatever. That's for the younger guys. The old guys sit out in the woods, drink clean, cool shine and call the shots. Sometimes somebody needs some serious work done, one of these semiretired guys'll take it because that's how you keep that kinda reputation."

Terry's face said she thought the game macabre. "For quality?"

"Top-drawer professional. Discreet, resourceful, committed. These aren't guys you rent to drop by and talk. Let's say, it's almost unheard of."

"You seem to know a lot about these people."

I wasn't sure if she missed the point or dodged it. Either way, I didn't see it worth pursuing. It was just a funny loose thread. I was alive because somebody didn't want to have to kill Terry. They did me, they'd have to do her to keep her from going to the cop house and talking. Maybe I should just count my blessings.

"Yeah. Too much, unfortunately. I know this: they won't talk anymore. You and I don't duck out, forget the whole thing, we become business. It's a firm message." I gave it some elbowroom, said, "Time to cut bait and run, baby?" I let my hands slide off the back of her seat, touched her with a fingertip. "You say it, I'm done."

That must have made its own elbowroom. She looked through the windshield.

I said: "Am I done?"

A quick wag of the head; a quiet, "No. It has to stop here. It has to stop with me."

I nodded nearly sagely, looked where she was looking, said, "I don't have the slightest idea what you're talking about."

"Me either, Sloan."

I huffed a couple of times, rearranged my ass. I think I said "Shit" under my breath. Then, I said, "Where are you staying?"

"A friend's. Why?"

"Anybody besides me and this friend know where you are?"

Terry thought about it. "No."

"Be sure, goddammit."

"I'm sure." The green eyes were looking in me. "You're not walking away, are you?"

"Hell, no, I'm not walking. I'll walk away when I'm outta the game, and I'm not outta the game yet." I didn't think I was. Something would come up. Something brilliant. Sure it would.

"Keep the money. Walk away." We had a new face up, a new Terry. "I'll handle it."

"Come on, Terry. Don't go sentimental on me. The city cops'll run me down anyway. I'm pretty heavily anted in the pot."

"Why would the city cops be looking for you?"

I smiled like I sold flowers. "The guy that died? I held him by his ankles for a little bit yesterday."

She rolled her eyes and leaned back on the inside of the door. "I don't know when you're kidding and when you're serious." A deadpan stare. "Do you? Do you know when to tell yourself it's just a game? When it's time to step off?"

"No, I don't. Do you?"

She went lateral. "So what are you going to do? How does Sloan play this out?"

"I need another list."

"The mobsters take it?"

Mobsters. "Yeah. Can you fax it to me with your cell?" I didn't think the game was so high-tech anyone might lift my phone calls but nowadays you never know. They could lift her cell number, but not her whereabouts.

She looked at me like I was dim-witted. Maybe she had something. "*Mais oui, mon cheri.*" I was being laughed at. "With my laptop. I could E-mail you."

"It wouldn't do us any good."

A smile. "You don't have a computer."

"Oh, I have one. We're just not on real familiar terms."

"You've never been online, have you?"

"Online? Sweetheart, I'm not even sure what a Palm Pilot is."

"The list will be on your fax when you get home." It was.

I grabbed a bucket of chicken on the way in, put it on my little Formica table, got ketchup and Crystal hot sauce and the fax. The list wasn't telling me anything new.

I found the one I'd talked Billy Joe and Stiff out of and unrolled it. Side by side, I started playing around, trying to match up real names with the Gallic zoo. With one set of phone numbers covered, I got a few, even with my limited command of French. I knew *Lapin* was rabbit. Hooked it up with a guy named Roger. *Buffle* sounded like buffalo and I gave it to an eastern name. I was right. That was it. I got my pen out and began inadvertently completing the matchup.

I was cooling my mouth down with Newcastle, dipping fried chicken in liquid fire, when it occurred to me I couldn't match them up. Terry's list had eighteen. Grady's had seventeen.

Well, fucking yes, dumb-ass. The naughty client wouldn't

have his nickname and phone number out there. I did a quick matchup. Who's on Terry's list that isn't on the other? A guy named Randy Brian. The Brain. Well, eu-fucking-reka. Maybe Grady did know his partner's name. The stoners said Grady called his guy "The Brain."

I rung Terry. No answer. I left a message: *Call*.

Wonder if Randy Brian knew Grady was dead? Wonder if Randy knew he was next? Or would he be? Could the hillbilly cowboys know Brian was the one making the calls if Grady didn't know? But if Grady didn't know the name was Brian, why did he call him the Brain?

I didn't waste much gray stuff on it. Grady said something to Stiff and Billy Joe about following his guy around; maybe he got lucky. I dialed Randy Brian's number.

"Web Tech. How may I direct your call?" A fucking ISP. No wonder the guy turned to blackmail.

"Where are you located?"

The voice told me. Shyster's Row up in Altamonte. I asked if Randy was in and when she connected me we got cut off. Or maybe I hung up. I didn't want to have phone over this. Neither would Randy, I wouldn't guess. I did him a favor, drove down to see him, see if we might discuss his impending murder face-on.

The place was about as you'd expect an Internet anything these days, but no one had asked for the furniture back yet. Not bad in a warehouse, Rooms To Go sort of way. A brunette with access to cosmetics sat behind half a grainy transaction window. She was pecking away and said, dripping with insincerity, one word: "How-may-I-help-you?" She sounded like she wished I had a straight razor to my throat. Then she'd help me.

"Mr. Brian, please."

"Is-he-expecting-you, Mr. . . . ?"

"Mr. Jones. About the Sebring account."

Something snagged. "I don't recall a Sebring account."

"Randy will." It must have been my self-confidence. She smiled.

"You think so?" She was looking for some fun. The pecking stopped.

"Uh-huh. And watch his face when you say it."

She watched me some more. "Okay," and she was gone.

I didn't fend for myself too long before she brought the smile back in. It had turned mischievous. "You were right."

"About the account?" I knew what she meant.

"No. His face."

I nodded, standing on a smile. "He want to see me?"

Her eyebrows danced. "Oh, yes. Third door on the left. Have fun."

"I will."

Randy Brian had a nice office full of more rent-to-own stuff and a good view of the building across the way. The walls were covered in photographs. Mountains, rivers, vistas. A few snaps of people, but mostly things viewed from a distance. Looked like he had a hobby. There was one of those caricatures on the wall. The guy in it was drawn with an oversized head. It was entitled *The Brain.* Looked like I was in the right place.

The Brain sat behind a neat desk and smiled at me. He had my number. He was going to chew me up and spit me out and not get a dribble on his chalk-striped suit. I found a seat.

"Well, you're about what I'd expect."

He looked like he liked to talk. I let him have at.

"I heard there was somebody shaking her contacts down."

I sat some more while he stood, showing me what an important piece of real estate he was.

"Well, whatcha getting a piece? No pun." He liked his own jokes.

Randy Brian was heavy-jowled, maybe fifty. Average body but legs that jacked him up disproportionately to six-eight or so. Chrome-domed with a rusty fringe sporting enough slickum to make it mind its manners all the way down past his shirt collar. Good old Randy Brian. Networking son of a gun.

And then here comes Sloan to fuck up a three-martini lunch. "Grady Pelham's dead, Randy."

Nothing changed in his big jowly face but his eyes. They went from beady to pitiful. It was quite touching. Over a paralyzed smile, he said, "Say what?"

The sad-sack face with the lost-boy sag to it, I had to laugh a little. Put it on Randy's tab.

"Crazy game, huh? One day you're eating the bear; next day the bear's eating you." I had my face calmed down to a smile. "So whatcha gonna do now?"

"About what?" Randy was going cagey again. I'd better watch myself.

"About not ending up like Grady. And don't insult me with any sales talk. You're scrambling for your life here, Randy." I gave him some faux sympathy. "Unless, of course, you wanna go to the cops, tell them about taking pictures and making phone calls."

"Who are you and who killed Grady Pelham?"

Just the facts, huh? At least we got past the denial phase pretty quick. "I'm a friend of 'her'. I don't know who killed Grady, but I've got a good idea. And if you wanna plan your future beyond dinner, you'd better talk to me, Randy. Did Grady know your real name?"

"Why?"

"If he didn't, you might get to live another thirty, forty-five minutes. Did he?"

Brian shook his head. "No. He left a message here one night. On the machine, goddam idiot. From what he said, I knew he was looking for me. I called him back. My friends call me The Brain, so I used that." I wondered why anyone would call this guy The Brain. Maybe his friends were dumbfucks too.

"If you guessed, how would you say Grady found the opportunity to meet his demise?"

A hand shined the bald region of the head once. "Someone was dropping some money last night."

"You guys have much luck at this? I mean, before this time?"

"Some. Three guys paid up. Small amounts." He shrugged. "Times are hard in a lot of industries. The market sucks." His face looked like he was trying to borrow money.

"How many you contact?"

"Eight. The first nine, minus the fifth one. He's dead. Too much drinking and driving. Damn. This is bad."

No shit. "Who was he meeting?"

Brian looked at the spotless blotter on his desk. He was down. "I don't know."

It sounded wrong. "Excuse me?"

"Okay." He was up. "The three that paid, I knew who they were. This one I didn't. I left a cell phone number when I called if I got an answering machine. He called the cell."

I interrupted. "What did caller ID say about him?"

"Local."

"You check the number?" I knew the answer.

"Yes. Pay phone."

"Some guy calls you up, from a pay phone, wants to make you rich. Didn't hit you as odd?"

"Yes. It spooked me a little but hey, this player wanted the

75

whole list. Put a fantastic number on it. Super offer. Absolutely super. All we do is meet, sign some papers, we get a suitcase full of money."

"So why didn't you make it? Run outta nerve?"

"Yes. Yes I did. I was more afraid of the police showing up than . . . this."

"So. You going to the cops or do you wanna help me narrow the field a bit?"

He studied me, the Dale Carnegie parked. "Do I have any choice?"

"Not that I see. Maybe if you ran out that door and kept running. Unless the boys who did Grady are sitting on your front fender when you get to your car. Besides that, no, Randy, I don't see you facing many choices."

"You think if I stick around, these people will find me?"

"I did and I'm not Dick Tracy. They've got one of those pieces of paper I was holding when I figured it out. Took mine. And unless Grady figured the other piece was worth his life, I expect they have them both. The ones I met seemed a little homespun but they didn't seem stupid. Yeah. I'd say just a matter of time. Hell, Randy, they may find you anyway, even if you leave right this red-hot."

"Grady had a copy of the list?"

"Uh-huh."

"How did he get his hands on it?"

"Goddam, Randy, how the fuck would I know? I'd say he swiped it from you."

"I can't believe that thieving lowlife."

"Yeah, that's a heartbreaker. It's getting to where you can't trust anyone to do the right thing. Even high-caliber folks like Grady. You know what Grady's friends and associates called him?"

"No." His face wasn't having much fun.

"Shady Grady. Think they were just fooling around, putting the handle on it because it rhymed? Sounded cute?"

His face was in his hands, and I could see freckles on his scalp. "Looks like I misjudged the market."

"Misjudged? You don't have the slightest idea what the fuck's going on. You'd better wake up, pal."

"Cut my losses?"

"I think you're a little late for any spin. You're down to two options. Me, or the cowboy hats."

"What's your deal?"

"I'll get you outta here, outta the building. You keep going. Don't come back. Ever. Deal?"

"Not even if I give you my information? I can't come back? Even after things ease down?"

"Never, Randy. You got a guy killed. You stick around till the cops grab me? I'll give your ass up so fast, you'd think you'd always been in jail. All I'm doing for you, and that's against my better judgment, is seeing your miserable ass to the interstate. If that doesn't seem like a viable option, you're on your own right now."

The guy never stopped playing. "Listen." He looked around like we were in a crowded restaurant and some of Bill Gates's spies were watching. "There's another angle to this thing. You interested? I need some help working it. Super opportunity."

A head wag coming from incredulous was all I had for that. "You heard the offer, Randy. Take it; leave it. It's all the same to me."

"You know who she is, friend? Nineteen sixty-four, sixty-five, her family sold over twenty thousand acres to the attraction people at one shot. That's a lot of real estate, friend." He was wearing a salesman face.

"I'm not your friend, Randy. You fuck with Terry or her

family, I'll break your goddam legs. I didn't hear you say where you were on the offer I made."

Randy must have been tired of Orlando. "I'll take it." He turned and clicked a mouse a few times. A printer at his elbow woke and spit out a sheet of paper with French words on it. I'd seen it; I had one just like it.

Randy took a pen and boxed and struck and circled. He shoved it at me. "The guys in that box, I called. The one guy struck through, he's dead. The three I circled paid up."

"How much did you get?" It didn't matter; I was just curious.

He made a face. "Diddly. Two grand from one guy. A grand from another. The third guy cried. I mean, actually cried. Came up with eight hundred bucks. The others, I just assumed they didn't care who knew they consorted with prostitutes. They never called back."

"Makes you wonder what ever happened to morality, doesn't it, Randy?"

Randy agreed. He asked if he could zip his files before we left and I told him to zip away. He zipped and we set up the Terry thing in reverse. I left first and gave him a place nearby to pull over so I could get between his worthless ass and my friends in the Lincoln should they be skulking about.

I waited for fifteen minutes. I never laid eyes on Randy "the Brain" Brian again. At the time, I thought maybe he'd wised up enough to make a run for his life.

FOURTEEN

For a few days the birds sang, the grass grew and the sun showed up enough to keep its pension plan intact. I had told Terry to hang low for a couple of more days. Told her I owed her a few grand back. She said not to worry my pretty little head.

Man, I love this fucking country. Where else could a guy with no motivation, no goals, no expectations knock down fifteen large, minus a few Franklins tossed at expenses, in a couple of short days?

Third day, I'm lying around letting the sun shine on the bottoms of my feet, feeling too smart, too pretty and too proud. I've been to the shop enough times I should know what that shit gets you.

In my case, it got me the first of several disturbing phone calls that came within the hour. Everything was looking good; the sky fell.

First ring, Terry Sebring.

"Good morning, Red." The guy who invented caller ID should get the Nobel. A beautiful blow for antisocialism.

"Have you seen the paper?"

My business, that's never a good question. At best, it means the cops did for free what you couldn't do for money. At worst, you get to look down and see your pants around your ankles. I ended up closer to the pants-around-the-ankles side.

"Where am I looking?" I was grabbing newspapers.

"Today. B section. Page one, first."

Oh good. Multiple articles. I caught the first one. A local businessman had been shot while jogging in Al Coith Park.

Unknown assailant. Nobody saw dick. Nobody heard dick. Every day for four years, Richard David Frazier, fifty-eight, had jogged the same route. A neighbor said he was a nice man and always spoke. He was a paying member of one of the taller steeples downtown. It listed his relatives who had, along with everyone else in Orlando, survived what the cops called a random act.

We knew him.

"The list, right?"

"Yes. Second page, same section."

Another local had been mowed down two days back in a hit-and-run affair at a parking garage. Another name we knew. Nadir Ramdi. Dr. Ramdi. Did something at the geek park by the University, according to the paper. The buffalo, according to my memory.

"I remember this one. You got ideas? Why these two?"

"They were the first two locals in my Palm Pilot."

I thought about it. "What were these guys?"

"Autruche and *Buffle."*

"Who's next? That list."

"Let's see. Local. Randy Brian, but he's gone, right?"

"I hope. Now I'm beginning to wonder."

"He wouldn't be that stupid, would he?" Of course he would.

My telling him to beat it was for my conscience alone. He passed on the advice? Fuck him. "You know him better than I do. Whadda you think?"

She didn't make me feel any better about it. "He likes himself."

"You hear from him, let me know. Better yet, pass him on to me."

"If he's back, won't the"—Terry looked for a word that didn't start with killers—"the people who are doing this find him?"

"Maybe not. He took his name off the copy Grady was

working on. It's on the other one, though. Who knows? Sounds like they're working off Grady's list right now." I had a big idea. "Hang on."

I went inside and found the faxed list from Terry, and the Randy Brian version. I checked the latter. Fucking chump luck. Both guys who had bought it were circled. They had paid up. The other pay-up was circled near the bottom of the box of nine Randy Brian said he contacted.

I named off the nine in the box, minus two dead good-faith boys and one been-dead guy. "Who lives here, outta the six left?"

"Three. Sam Bardicello, restaurants and restaurant supply. Davis Cambridge, lawyer. Rembert Gordon."

Rembert didn't need an intro. He was a local television fakir with a big pile of concrete that had a cross on top of it out toward the fantasy. Rembert railed against vileness. Demon alcohol. Demon nicotine. Demon queers. Demon working mothers. Good tolerant Christian boy who would lay hands on your sinful ass, you didn't watch it. Did real well at the shell game. Then, Rembert had a vision. It said to taketh equal parts of thy ministry and of thy capitalism and buildeth a theme park unto the lord. Rembert's bounty increaseth faster than the pope's these days.

I let Rembert go, grabbed another name I'd heard before. I played dumb. "Tell me why the name Bardicello rings a bell."

A little hesitation. "He's supposed to be connected."

Connected to what? "Yeah? What's his take on this little game?"

"He says he doesn't care. I believe him. His wife's dead and he's pretty wide open. Sam even called and offered to take care of the situation for me. Do you think it's one of those three?"

"Just playing around with something Randy told me. How about the lawyer? He keep a machine gun in his briefcase?"

She laughed. "No. He's my oldest client. He does land acquisition. Quite harmless."

"Good. It'll make up for the other two."

"You have to go see them?"

"I'm thinking on it. Maybe Sammy Boy since it looks like he's next up. I've got another idea too." It related to seeing Sammy but I didn't mention it.

"The police?"

"Not yet. Depends on how today goes."

Hesitation. "Sloan?"

"Yeah?"

"Is it time to step off? Let the police have it?"

"Not yet, Red. Even if the cops fucked up and caught the Dixie boys, they'd get *nada* out of them. Those boys would shut their mouths and do their time."

She didn't understand what that was about. "Why not?"

"Honor, sweetheart. So old and passed-down nobody knows why anymore. These guys just do it."

"Spooky bunch."

"Tell me." And I was the guy who was going to see if he could find them. Terry and I exchanged wishes of luck and I read the two articles again. I hadn't flushed up much emotion over Shady Grady. Too much irony. The two new dead guys bothered me. I don't know if I could have done anything about it. I knew I hadn't. I could have called the cops and told them what I knew.

Then what? Things go chilly, the shooters go back to the hills, the guy writing the checks goes on like nothing ever happened. The cops come up with *nada* except me and Terry. Maybe a couple of knotheads who steal cars.

A week? A month? Another call from Terry that goes: Hey,

Sloan, check the B section; yeah, the elephant's dead. No. That wouldn't work.

I was way closer than the cops. If I could take the cowboys out of the mix, I figured I could do my short-list some justice. That was the trick. And if what Terry had said about Bardicello was straight, I had a trick. It was dirty as hell but it got me where I needed to be. Thinking about it didn't throw me into a crying jag, so I left it as an option.

That's as far as I got before I was looking at the little screen on the phone. Rachel Preston. I had a guess. I let it ring again.

"Yeah?"

"Mr. George?"

"Yeah, Rachel. How you doing?" The cards I dealt around at Billy Joe's place had the name John Paul George. It's not too original but it makes you smile.

"Okay, I guess." She wasn't okay.

I could hear the kooky music and voices of a kids' show. "You guys in a motel?"

"Yeah."

"What's wrong, Rachel?"

"Hang on." Offline, I could hear her asking Tammie to turn the television down. Tammie did what Mommy asked and Mommy said to me, "Billy Joe and Stiff left."

"What do you mean, left? Like, took off and aren't coming back and you're stranded, or like, went somewhere and didn't make it back?" I saw this shit coming at me. Too much cash had been passed around.

"They went back to Apopka."

I breathed deep. "They rocking it?"

"Uh-huh. Left last night. We got a motel cause the campground people got tired of Billy Joe and Stiff and the noise. And they brought that stupid kid who lives next door."

83

"Gerald?"

"Uh-huh. Anyhow, they bought a bunch o' rock with the money you give 'em. Last night around ten, they ran out and took off for home. They said they was comin' right back, but I ain't seen 'em since." Maybe she'd get lucky.

"They'll show. What're you people using for traveling money?" I knew.

"We used what you gave me. I hid a hundred, though."

"Billy Joe took the rest?"

"Uh-huh."

"Where are you?"

"Fernandina. The Hampton's Inn."

"And you've got a hundred cash?"

"Uh-huh."

"You and the kids enjoying yourselves?"

She cheered up. "Oh, yeah. They love it. Diggin' sand fleas. Playin' in the ocean. Makin' sand castles. Willie wants a surfboard cause he saw some cool guys surfin'."

"You still close to the beach?"

"Across the street. At least till noon. Then, I don't know. I guess we have to leave."

"No. You stay right there. Give me the number. I'll make arrangements with Mr. Hampton. And I mean this: you and those kids stay right there till *I* call. Need be, I'll get you home. Enjoy."

"Mr. George, why're you doin' this?"

I thought about it. I could have told her that the guys who wanted her worthless old man were good shots, way on out past a hundred yards even, and it might fuck the kids up to see Daddy's head explode like a watermelon in a microwave. I said, "I don't know," because that was closer to the truth.

I called the Hampton Inn and left them a credit card number, put a hundred cash on top of it. Fuck it. I was back

84

in business, and tossing other people's money around was one of my favorite parts of the business.

I'd hardly finished patting myself on the benevolent back when the last call came in. It was The Brain.

"Sloan, Randy Brian." Like we talked all the time. Like we were buds. Randy Brian, networking son of a gun.

All I could come up with was a laugh I reserve for rare occasions. Like maybe an absolute assault on Darwinism.

"Listen, I just got off the phone with Terry."

Fucking business. The guy's in the spider's web, and he's about to go business on me. "How much do you need, Randy?"

"She said you might have five laying around, ready to go."

I laughed again. I couldn't help it. "You know, Randy, you're outta your fucking mind. You gotta be."

"The five grand, chump. That's all I need from you."

"Listen, stupid. I'm gonna 'splain something to you slow. There are two lists. The other bad guys, not you and Grady, but the guys who are killing people? They got both lists. One has some French words and some phone numbers. Seventeen numbers. Then there's another one with real names on it. Eighteen names. Can you subtract, Randy?"

Maybe he couldn't; he didn't say.

"Let me help you. Eighteen minus seventeen equals one. One equals you, Brain. Bang, you're dead. Get the fuck outta town, Randy. I've warned you off twice now. You keep making these prank calls and you get dead? I'm okay with it. See you." I dropped the connect.

FIFTEEN

I called some people and promised them some things I'll have to deliver on someday. But I didn't have to sell my soul to come away with a few vitals on my shortlist.

Sam Bardicello was the hard one. Second call, I got someone to call me back and I gave them enough to get Sammy "the Fish" Bardicello's attention. And his attention got me an invite to a meet.

The Fish had a very nice house in a very nice neighborhood. New as invention, but nice with nice neighbors. Probably had him a ball chaser of one breed or another next door. Maybe a theme park executive or two. A vote chaser here and there. New money; no tolerance. Had a sign up telling you about it: no-tolerance zone.

The house was a big two-story stucco job, maybe tan, maybe gray. Tile roof patinaed to a suspicious perfection. The beds had a fussed-over look and probably drank a lot of water. The chemically addicted lawn, green as a Welsh poet's fuse, supported a few paranoid live oaks bowing away from the fickle Florida sky. Color jumped up around them.

A semicircular drive swung near the house, then around to avoid a detached garage. A big guy in a sport shirt with bulges was rinsing at a white Caddie without much enthusiasm. My arrival didn't seem to help. I gave him back the squint he was aiming at me.

The guy's squint had gone over to a sneer thing by the time

I was out of my car and I could tell he was waiting for me to ask him something so he could give me some cute shit he'd been saving up. I disappointed him and went for the front door.

"The fuck you goin'?"

I gave him a little grin. "You the butler?"

"Do I look like the butler?" The guy had a ponytail that shook when he talked.

"Nah. You got a decent Jersey accent, and you're supposed to look like muscle, but you gotta work the sneer if you're gonna sell it. Put some lip to it."

The guy didn't know where to go next and he wasn't fast enough to figure me for hired help, so he put his hands out and shrugged. "Hey, people come drivin' in here, don't know the people live here from nothin', know what I'm sayin'? I gotta ask who you are, why you're here, okay?"

"Fine. I'm Sloan. Your boss needed some help deciding what dress to wear today."

The guy was about to smile. "Okay. I get it. You're the dick. And a smart-assed motherfucker. You and the man in there may skin each other up some, dick." He was smiling now. "He don't like smart-asses."

"I'll keep that in mind."

He didn't say anything else; he just grinned like the joke was on somebody else. Like me, maybe.

A brick walk with some Aztec crap patterned into it took me to the front door. I ignored the doorbell and grabbed the ring in the brass lion's mouth and banged it loud enough.

The woman who answered was thin. She had a thin face with a thin nose over a thin mouth. She had thin ash blond hair that swung over one eye, and she looked up from under there to speak. "Yes?" I might have been boring her. I couldn't tell.

She was looking at me like she figured I was drumming up yard work. Maybe I did look that way. I was pretty dressed-down to be calling on a few million bucks, but I didn't want anyone to get the wrong impression.

"I'm Sloan."

Her mouth did something funny while her eyes did me, stopping at the wrong places to make me feel comfortable. The funny something went over to a smile. The smile confirmed my suspicions. I wasn't what she was expecting.

I must have passed as a reasonable facsimile of a PI; she crooked a finger at me and turned around and started down the hall. No tourists tolerated in this hood, so I left the sun on its own this time and followed her narrow fanny and thin ankles for a couple of miles to a door on the left. The room where she dumped me was all dark wood and maroon leather. The wood looked like it was older than Orlando; the leather could have been. It was supposed to look manly, and I guess it did.

I plowed across some Oriental rugs thrown this way and that, several layers deep, to a chair that looked like it wasn't too uncomfortable. I was wrong.

I looked at some books sitting in shelves along the walls. They looked old; some had leather spines. They could have been worth something. I didn't know. I'm not that smart. I did that for what seemed like fifteen minutes, then I checked the time. Both hands on eleven.

A couple of minutes later, I was trying to give my nuts some space in my pants, and a man with stiff hair came in. If he noticed me pulling at my crotch, he didn't mention it. I didn't mention the hair.

The Fish looked more like one of the vote chasers than a guy with seven or eight restaurants, some boats on each of Florida's coasts and some big ideas that were mostly about

88

moving on the Trafficante riffraff left in Tampa. White tennis stuff, a light sweater, blue, over the shoulders, tied under his chin. Some quality gold accentuation here and there, and not incredibly gaudy for a guy with a crew.

The appraisal of me was done in the walk across the room. It didn't look good. There was a big desk with nothing on it, a chair with a back that went up forever. He hooked a cheek on the corner of the desk. "You any good?"

"Depends on who you're asking."

He continued the study. "You've gotta be about the damnedest-looking pimp I ever saw. And I've seen some."

"Easy, Mr. Bardicello."

"Easy. Easy, he tells me. You got balls, mister. I'll give you that. Tell me one thing. Was this Terry's idea?"

"What?"

I wasn't making him happy. "Fuckin' what? Fuckin' comin' here and leanin' on me, for Christ sakes."

"Who's leaning? Not me. And you're insulting Terry if you think for a minute she doesn't wanna see this thing go away at least as badly as you do. Come on, you really don't look that stupid." He wasn't sure if I'd insulted him or not. He didn't kill me so I went back at him. "You trusted her, didn't you? One time?"

He was pissed and didn't want to play school. "Yeah. One time."

"You in the habit of trusting people who let you down?"

I had his attention. "Hell no." He turned, slid off the desk, and crossed to a little bar. "It's noon somewhere. Whatcha drinkin', Sloan? It's Sloan, right?"

"Yeah. Surprise me with anything but bourbon."

"You don't care for bourbon, Mr. Sloan?" Ice clinked.

"Not much. You know any guys who drink bourbon when

89

they're not nibbling shine? Wear cowboy hats and polyester suits? Red clay on their boots?"

Our eyes were talking if our mouths weren't while he hiked back from the bar. He sat mine down within arm's reach and didn't wait on me. It looked like a Collins and he dropped half of his. "Drink up."

I did. It was a Collins. A good one. "Straight talk?" I held my glass up.

He clinked me. "Straight talk."

We drank to it. I sat mine down as he turned to get another.

"I think you're in some pretty serious danger here. Tonight, tomorrow. Soon." For all the response I got, he might not have heard it.

He brought the fresh drink back and sat it on the desk untouched. The big chair was still there. He used it.

"We're not talking about egging my house here, right?" The guy had a subtle sense of humor.

"No. There's a list floating around. Terry's customers. Couple of guys on this list got horizontal in the last day or two. A midnight auto-parts guy who stumbled across the list got that way too." I gave him a beat and took my shot. "You didn't kill them, did you, Mr. Bardicello?"

It didn't even distract him. He was deep in thought, he flicked a hand at it. "No. Why am I next?"

"Your name's on the list. Right under the two dead guys."

We sat some, sipped some, then Sammy Bardicello showed me he wasn't a dull boy. "Okay, so some assholes get this list, get some entrepreneurial ideas, start callin' guys, askin' for dough. Yeah, okay, they called here. I told 'em to get lost. What do I give a shit? I'd go anywhere with Terry on my arm. I take her to nice places, we may do somethin' else, we may not. My age, whadda I care? And whadda I care

90

somebody tells somebody they seen me with a hooker? Fuck 'em.

"But somebody on this list ain't nearly so liberal as me, but he don't know who's doin' the callin'. He gets a big idea: Hey, maybe it's one of the customers." He hunched his shoulders, put his hands out, agreeing with himself. "So we start at the top of the list and now we're at Sam Bardicello. How's that?"

"Damn good. You left out a couple of details that take you from the grease monkey to the guy making the phone calls to the guy with the hired talent, but all told? Not bad. Consider yourself warned, Mr. Bardicello."

"Yeah. Thanks. And hey," I got a manicured finger pointed at me, "Sammy to you, ace. I'll keep my head down. Listen," the cobra said to the rat. "How's about a copy o' that list? I could get some boys to go visit these guys, figure out who's who. Whatcha say?"

"Nah, Sammy. I'm shortlisting now and if you're telling me you're not in there, it's getting shorter. You heard me about the cowboy hats, didn't you?"

Sammy gave me a grand jury smile. "You bet your ass I heard you. I know the kinda talent you're talkin'. I've had occasion." Sammy nodded, pensive. "Yeah, that's a clean piece of advice. I don't get much o' that. I owe you."

Yes he did. "Lemme ask you, Sammy; you guys have any cross-cultural exchange with those people?"

"If you're talking those Alabama yahoos, nah. We don't overlap much. Savannah, Gulf Coast, wherever you got your shipyards. We don't socialize, if that's what you're askin'. And we don't take no shit off 'em either."

"Like coming into your town with a kiss for you?"

"Yeah." I was getting the Fish. "Whatchu thinkin'?"

91

"Whatever may come up. I need a couple of sides of beef, can I call?"

"By all means. Who was the guy makin' the calls?"

I thought about it, put down some insurance. "A guy name Randy Brian. Internet guru. I ran him off, but he's back. You find him, he's your huckleberry."

Sammy rolled some eyes, shook an expensive haircut. "Fuckin' computer geeks. It ain't bad enough I gotta watch the tough guys. Russians. Albanians. Columbians. Even peckerwoods. Now I gotta watch out for fuckin' geeks." Then he nodded the haircut some. "I owe you, Sloan."

"Yeah." If I was lucky, that's how we'd leave it.

The thin woman's reappearance coincided so closely with my finishing the Collins, I wondered if there was a peephole behind a picture somewhere. Sammy and I swapped canned cordialities and the woman and I hit the trail for the front door.

She wasn't bad in a hungry, remote sort of way. A modern version of a torcher.

"You and Mr. Bardicello have a nice meeting?"

"Splendid. And it's Sammy to me, ace." I did a decent Sammy for her but my finger wasn't as well maintained as his. It brought me a smile.

"You're coming up in the world." She was being as serious as I was. "Don't be a stranger."

We were at the door now. She opened it. The sunshine had waited patiently for me, it looked like.

"Who would you be?"

The boldness in her eyes was distracting. "I'm Sammy's administrative assistant."

"What does an administrative assistant do?"

The bold eyes were playing with me. "Nothing like you're thinking, I'm sure."

92

"I wasn't thinking anything; I was just making conversation."

"Maybe you should." I got the bold eyes. "You get your nerve up, come by and see me. I'll give you something to think about."

SIXTEEN

Hanging around Sammy's little subdivided piece of Florida waiting for black Lincolns to show didn't pay squat, so I cruised over to Charlie Boscoe's and got the Jag. See if maybe it blended in a little better than my sled on these upscale streets. I spun around Sammy's neighborhood some more and still didn't spot any cowboys hats.

I crossed town and caught Sheeler Road and didn't spot any rednecks. No red-dirt cowboys, no rednecks. Nobody wants to play with Sloan.

Maybe Davis Cambridge, Esquire, wanted to play. I swung by my pad and called his office. Mr. Cambridge was busy in court now. Would I like to come by later this afternoon for a conference?

I told the voice on the other end of the line that would be just right. Then I shot the voice some baloney about property line disputes I was having with some imaginary neighbors. The voice shot me some baloney about how I had called the right place. I killed the conversation with expressions of gratitude and hung up.

Now I was bored. Maybe I should get out, go to a theme park. Maybe Touch Ministries: The Christian Experience. God knows, I could use it. I called Terry and asked her about a detail. A tiny little detail, innocent as a prybar.

"But you've got five of these shrouds. How do you know which one is real? How do you know any of them are real?"

The pimply boy in the fake Arab outfit was showing me his epiglottis.

"You got three Holy Grails, two Arks of the Covenant and seven Crowns of Thorns. All authenticated. Don't you think that's a little confusing to your average fundamentalist?"

The kid blinked a couple of times while his mouth balked at the gate. It didn't make him look any smarter. When he recovered, he tossed me some canned stuff. "Touch Ministries obtains any and all available antiquities of the one God and his beloved Son, Jesus of Nazareth. The goal is by obtaining any and all. . . . " He ran out of cue cards.

"Antiquities."

"Yeah, antiquities." He did a little head bounce, mouthing it, found his place. " . . . antiquities available, the ministry can guarantee the Christian public a degree of. . . . "

"Authenticity?"

"Nah. Something like security or something."

"You don't really know, do you?"

The kid was disappointed in himself. "No sir, but it goes like, You can be more sure that we got the real stuff than other similar facilities do."

"That's good, Darin. You can go catch the group again." Someone behind me spoke. Someone with some ass, if Darin's face was any gauge.

Darin said yes'm then nodded and mumbled at me and went to catch the herd I'd cut him out of. He did it all in one move and was glad to be putting terrazzo between me and him.

When he was clear, the voice behind me said, "Was there something you were in search of besides salvation?"

"Maybe some redemption." I turned. "Do I get that in the gift shop on the way out?"

The voice had told me she would be worth looking at. It didn't tell me she was exotic. Nor tall. Nor nearly perfect. The honey-streaked hair of the French-Asian encounter. Perfect almond eyes the color of bitter chocolate. Perfect cheekbones set high and proud. Most of her was set high and proud.

Yeah. She would have been perfect, from the single pearl at her neck to the diaphanous print silk blouse to the no-bullshit straight-line skirt and down to a pair of sensible shoes. Except the nubbly tan cashmere jacket over it all was asymmetrical. There was a bulge, left side, low. About cross-draw height. But like I say, besides that? She was perfect.

"Redemption's always included in the season ticket package. But you're just a day-tripper, aren't you?" I would have placed her late twenties. She was such a dish, it didn't matter.

We were having fun. "Yeah."

"How much of this do you believe?" Maybe a test.

"You mean this right here? Inside this fence, or the whole concept?"

"The concept. That's good. I like that." I got some eyes I would have dived into. "Would your answer to either be much different?"

I didn't need long. "No. Not much."

"I didn't think so. In that case, what are you looking for?"

"A lost soul."

"You'd be better served at the service Sunday morning."

Our primal versions were circling each other.

"I don't think this particular lost soul would want to talk

about what I wanna talk about at Sunday service." Circle some. She could see it coming.

"And where did this soul get lost?" Prybar time.

"Till maybe a month ago, fourth floor, Peabody Hotel, second Thursday each and every month."

Damn, she could play poker. Even the nearly amused smile hanging tough. She found a tiny phone in a coat pocket, used it to say: "I'm off-property for a bit. Code seven-three."

She pointed with the phone and we used a door for employees only. I followed her for a few turns and didn't mind the view at all.

The lady pushed a door and sunshine came in at an early afternoon angle. We both had shades and used them. I looked over and she had an electronic key up. A four-year-old BMW talked back and clicked its door locks in glee.

Over the top of the car, I asked, "What's code seven-three?"

"Going off-site to get something to eat besides the shit they serve in the canteen."

I put my grinning face in the hot car. She used a back gate and we were headed north, the open windows yanking the heat out.

Windows up and AC cranked, she said, "What's your name?"

"Sloan. What's yours?"

"Lee. Sarah." Pause. "Don't say it. My parents were immigrants. They didn't realize they were naming me after a cupcake."

"Okay." I didn't poke fun. Hell, I thought it was nice.

"We have people who show up asking for or demanding money. Not all nice stories. But you don't fit that. What's your play?"

My play? I might fall in love, a woman talks like that. "No play. Just a warning."

A bit of alarm gave itself away. "From who? You?"

The way she said it didn't make me sound very dangerous. Or even smart.

"Not from me, I assure you. How about I buy you late lunch and tell you a story that'll make you think about Pandora's box."

"You haven't eaten either?"

"Not unless they've added Tom Collins to the food groups since I got outta school."

"Rembert's got something for that. Sure cure."

"I bet. Come with the season pass?"

"No, it's extra."

Sarah Lee found a strip center and pulled up in front of a sign with a picture of a rack of balls and a couple of cue sticks. Next door was a trendy little place named after some French bread. The cupcake took me into the pool hall.

We settled on nachos, hot wings, potato skins, shit like that. Bar food. No Newcastle but plenty of Harp, which works any day.

I racked them up and watched her kick my ass. I might as well have been Stevie Wonder for all the shots I was allowed. I'm not Willie Mosconi but I think I chalk a fair stick. The lady embarrassed me. I had plenty of time to tell her the story. Once or twice she stopped me for clarification.

We moved to a big, hard plywood booth when the food came. I watched her pull on the Harp. "So you work for the prostitute."

"Yeah."

"Where are the local authorities?"

"Scratching ass."

I could tell that was okay with her team. "Do you plan on keeping it that way?"

I shrugged. "I think I'm doing better than they could on

this thing. Somebody else falls down, I don't know." I had a shrug and I tossed it in for free.

"You didn't say who was on your shortlist."

"No. I didn't."

"Are you going to?" She was making promises with her eyes I didn't think she'd keep.

"No."

"Is Rembert on it?"

"Yes."

We put on our nothing faces. Showed them to the other. Her face looked nice with nothing on.

"Would it do any good to ask if Rembert or anyone in his outfit would think any of this was worth fussing over?"

"There was talk. When the call came in."

"Talk among your people?"

"Me and Rembert and my boss, Ross Grace."

"Any talk about killing anyone?"

"No. We talked about damage control. What ifs. How much we could afford."

"Just curious. What would you have gone?"

"A million three."

"I know a guy named Randy would be very disappointed to hear such a figure. What happened?"

"He never called back."

"So far as you know."

She flushed a little. "Yes. So far as I know."

"How about Ross Grace? That his real name or did it come with the head centurion outfit?"

I got a nice shrug from a nice set of shoulders and a smile that said she was loosening up. "Ross talks tough, plays the Nam vet card well, but I don't find him particularly threatening. He's sort of Goody Two-Shoes."

I was shocked. "How about the chief forehead slapper?"

"Rembert? Jeez, he won't go to the bathroom unless some-one's waiting to do the heavy work for him. Six days a week, Rembert's about as active as a slug; he just leaves a slimier trail. He's a little boy with grown-up hormones."

"He ever hit on you?"

"Usually not more than once or twice a week." A shrug. "He knows how far to push it. Rembert's fat and lazy, but he knows his flock."

I added it up. "So your people are just waiting on a phone call? Give someone a nice piece of money?"

Sarah turned her head and looked across her eyes at me. "Don't make me sorry I told you that."

"Don't worry about it. Matter of fact, if the guy calls back, save your money."

"Why's that?"

I gave her a grin worth five bucks. "He won't be alive long enough to pick it up he doesn't stop making naughty phone calls."

The AC lay down, but Sarah Lee's BMW got us back to Wacko World and she dropped me at my car. I asked her if she liked to bowl and she said no. I said good, neither did I. Would she like to go to a nice joint for dinner tonight?

The nicest joint she could think of was her place in Delaney Park. I agreed sight unseen. Seven was good. Seven was perfect.

I did everything but click my heels as I unlocked my car. Anybody watching me would have run for the ticket window, got themselves $35 worth of what I had.

SEVENTEEN

Davis Cambridge had a high-ceilinged suite in convenient proximity to the new courthouse. A couple of walls had some tricky crap made of different exotic plywood panels. If it was art, there was no one there to tell me about it. The other walls had pictures hung on them. No one showed to tell me about those either.

I walked in ten minutes early and hadn't seen a living body since. Now I was on time.

With impeccable timing and all the affection of a mechanical dog, a face appeared at a break in the wood.

"Mr. Bonefy?"

"Yes."

"This way, please."

I went that way. Behind a serious young man of twenty-eight or so. I guess to what was their interpretation of a greenroom. Coffee, tea, doughnuts and *Why are you wasting our valuable, billable minutes?*

I was representing out-of-town interests who had gotten a survey that said the place next door had put the corner of their building on my guy's property. The clerk was so interested, he put his thumbs behind his tacky suspenders and practiced his judicious nod on me.

"And how did you come to us?"

By car? By guile? Take your pick. "A friend. I'd rather not

101

drop a name. I'll tell Mr. Cambridge should he require. He came highly recommended, though."

The guy was a little suspicious, but that was his job. He was a screen. And, I don't know what a land acquisition guy looks like, but I'm sure I wasn't looking the part. Not unless they're partial to knit silk sports shirts and well-trained fatigues.

The up-and-coming young man excused himself and his legal pad. All I told him, he could have written on his palm.

He returned in a few minutes with an apologetic look in tow. "Mr. Cambridge is still with a client. Would you care to see one of his associates?"

"Tell Mr. Cambridge I'm representing Terry Sebring." It got me nothing more than a momentary stumble.

"I'm sure that will mean something to Mr. Cambridge." It sounded like a question.

"I'm sure."

Young Clarence Darrow made another round trip, grabbed me on the back leg, and we went off arm in arm across knee-deep carpet the color of mulberries. A couple of miles up a hall, I was dumped in another office.

Davis Cambridge had a better view than Randy Brian. A nice scape of Orlando's tender, fresh skyline. A young girl coming of age. Concrete ribbons hauling neighbors out of the Land of Mordor and home to their own little fantasies. Water and glass and concrete and asphalt, moving under a million and a half tramping feet. The big parking lot.

I enjoyed the view for a bit, enjoyed Davis's chair. Enjoyed some pictures on the walls, some diplomas. Right before I got giddy, Davis Cambridge, Esquire, showed.

He didn't look so good. Maybe he'd had a long day in the trenches. His hair was in good shape as was his dark tailored suit. He had a good shine on his wing-tips. But, damn it, something wasn't right.

I guess that would be me, standing in his office.

"Sit down. This isn't a social call." Something about him was familiar and I wondered if I'd seen him before.

He was born here. Within fifty miles of where we were standing. I'd have bet on it. Dirt road twang, nearly nasal when he was irritated. Sixty-five? Give or take. Small, compact man with sandy hair shot with gray. Brows to go with the hair, hazel eyes to go with the brows. Pissed-off little old boar hog.

"Whatcha here for – what's your name? Bonefy?"

"No."

That stopped him. Momentarily. "Oh. So now you're comin' in heah, fraudulently passin' ya'self off as someone else? That it?"

He better lay off. I might crack and admit to the Lindbergh kidnap.

"You come in heah lookin' for a handful o' money, you messed up, boy. You just about to have the po-leece called on you. You hear me?"

I heard him but I acted like I didn't.

"You hear me? Want me to call the po-leece?"

I stood, spun the phone console on his desk. I punched zero, said, "Yeah. Junior. Get the Orlando Police Department on the line."

I looked at the dead receiver, looked at the Esquire. "Damn. He hung up on me. Should I dial out direct?"

"Sit down." Davis Cambridge had changed faces while I was on the phone. "Whadda you want? How much?" His new face said he was either tired or irritated. Probably both.

I wagged my head. "Mr. Cambridge, you wouldn't believe how many times lately I've been asked that. And you wouldn't believe what I could have knocked down if I had been smart enough to take them all up on it."

There was a tap at the door, it clicked behind me. Cambridge flapped a hand, said, over my head. "It's fine. I'll buzz, I need you." The door clicked again. "So you're not heah to shake me down?"

"No."

"Okay. I'll bite. Then why are you heah?"

"I'm sure you're aware someone has a list of Ms. Sebring's associates, making phone calls, demanding money."

"Yes. I've talked to this character. And you say you're representing Ms. Sebring?"

"Yeah. Name's Sloan."

"You doin' any good?"

"Not much."

"Then you had a reason for comin' by."

"Just letting you know, someone may be stalking some people on that list." Goddam, why didn't I just say watch out for the fucking bogeyman?

"If you're talking about the two dead gentlemen, I don't believe that falls under stalking, son. I talked to Ms. Sebring earlier. She didn't mention anything about you." He gave that some attention and a wrinkled brow. "Listen, I appreciate the warnin' and all your hard work, but don't you think you're a little over your head in this deal, friend? Outta your game?"

"You saying go to the cops?"

He shrugged it off. "Well? Eventually, aren't you goin' to have to?"

"Yeah. Eventually. I thought if I got rid of the phone caller, maybe things would settle down. I ran him off."

"Well, he's back. Called here, last time, about an hour ago."

"What are you gonna do?"

"I don't know, son. I may pay him a little. He's callin' back tonight."

"I'd advise you not to pay him."

"Why's that?"

"He's bluffing. He's on the dodge and he's running scared."

"Scared of what, son? You? The law?"

"Right now? This moment? I think I'm the least of that man's worries, Mr. Cambridge."

He didn't ask why; he asked: "What's the fella's name, Mr. Sloan?" Davis Cambridge had a legal pad too. He had a pen worth a couple of grand poised over it.

When I didn't respond, he moved the eyes from the pad to me. "He does have a name?"

"Of course. Why would you need it?"

The pen might have been made of nitroglycerin. He placed it gently on the pad, aligned it perfectly.

"A man hangs around the courthouse long enough, he ends up with a few friends in law enforcement might owe him a favor or two. A man like that might get one o' the people that owe him to go have a serious talk with this man. Convince him of his foolishness."

"This man's friends, the ones in law enforcement that owe him? They wouldn't feel like the job description demanded they look into a few dead people who happened to be involved?"

"Who says those people are involved? An unlicensed keyhole peeper? A whore? Who else? Not me, not anybody I know. You got any proof besides a list of names? That's why we got the word 'coincidence.' Shit does happen."

"Yeah. Happens all the time. Consider yourself advised." I'd had enough three-fifty an hour bullshit; I got up.

"And consider yourself advised. Don't mess around and let your pursuit of a few dollars get you in trouble, boy. Greed's a terrible master."

"I'll keep an eye on myself." No way I would walk before the eagle flew.

"And I could tell you about how a man like me could make life intolerably uncomfortable for a man in your line. How, a couple of phone calls, you'd have a big black *X* painted on you." His hand went to a drawer. A touch rolled it open on high-tech bearings. "But you know what I think you'd listen to better?" I knew. What he thought anyway.

"I don't want your money, Mr. Cambridge. I don't like what you think it might buy for you. Keep your head down."

I made it to the big solid wood door. "A thousand for the man's name. Another thousand for you to give me a daily update. That make you feel dirty, Mr. Sloan? I mean, isn't that what you do? Sell people, make reports?"

"Yeah. When I'm not dodging subpoenas and left hooks, or cleaning other people's shit off my shoes." I turned back and smiled for the contrite little bastard. "What would you do for two grand, Mr. Cambridge? Maybe get outta bed in the morning?"

"Maybe. But I ain't you, son. And you ain't me."

"I'll take the compliment and breeze before it goes bad. Good luck to you, sir."

"Same, son."

The oddest thing, I think we both meant it.

EIGHTEEN

Was I the only chump in town smart enough to be nervous? Seemed like it. Back at the shack, pushing the day around, that's all I could see. Lay it out this way; lay it out that way. Nobody was worried. Not enough for me.

Sure, Sammy "the Fish" Bardicello had a crew around him. Big, stupid magillas with guns. But he knew about red-dirt hit men. Up close, far away, car bomb, hit-and-run. They didn't give a shit. He seemed more preoccupied than anything.

The cupcake and her blessed crowd couldn't see why a big pile of dough wouldn't be fine. I'm sure they'd had success with that trick, and any good security team has to deal with that sort of nonsense from time to time. I'm sure the Elmer Gantry game's no different.

No. They would just keep Rembert in a jar until Sunday, bring him out, spray paint him, send him onstage to take care of the Lord's business. Probably the funniest part was, it might work fine. Cold as they might seem, I didn't see two good old hard-shell Baptist boys taking anyone out in church. Now, out walking around the church? Watch your ass.

Then Davis Cambridge, Esquire. His answer to everything was a check for a grand. Hey, hold on, boys, let me cut you a check; a thousand each work? Right, Davis. Those boys throw the safety, you're dead. And what good is arrogance and authority when you're dead?

At least Billy Joe and Stiff had narcotic addiction to blame. Dumb fucks.

That made me look at the message messiah. It was winking at me, so I poked a button.

Terry was just checking in.

Rachel hadn't seen her husband.

Sarah Lee wondered if I could pick her up at the service garage. Seems the AC on her car was going out. I would have picked her up on the Pan-American Highway in Costa Rica had she asked.

Randy Brian had called in a counteroffer, a super deal. Absolutely super. He knew I'd be interested. He was wrong.

Terry answered in a good mood and we chatted about the day, about the short-listers. The Brain.

"Are you still convinced it's one of those three?"

"It's not Brian. That's just *so* not him. Any of the other three? Sure. I'm with you on Sammy, though. I don't see him giving a shit. But who knows, Terry? You shove a wiseguy, he might react funny. So I'm still on three. And your little lawyer buddy is harmless like a water moccasin."

Terry laughed. "Oh, he's just bluffing. He try to buy you? Insult your ethics?"

"Among other things. I see him as someone willing to throw money at a situation. That's all it takes for what's going on."

"Trust me. His bark is much worse than his bite. He's just an ornery old man. His wife is infirm. Has been as long as I've known him. Nearly ten years now? Yes, that long."

"Well, nobody's out till they're dead in this game. Did you mention me to Cambridge?"

"No. Why do you ask?"

"No particular reason." Except for something he said, something he'd let slip and a couple of things he didn't say.

I got some soft sigh. "When? When does life get normal again?"

How about: maybe never. "Two days. It's over or I go to the cops with what I got. But I see it playing out fast from here."

"Who else is going to die?"

Maybe Billy Joe and Stiff. I didn't know why Randy Brian wasn't dead already. Who knows? Sammy? The preacher? Mean old Davis Cambridge? "No one, I hope. Terry, I'm doing the best I can here. I've warned off people I really didn't feel like warning off. I warned off two guys today who are in serious danger and talked to one who's killing people. All I gotta do is figure out who the fuck is who."

"And I know you will. I'm just getting cabin fever. Dinner tonight, no strings, no business?"

Drought, then rain. "I'm meeting someone tonight. One of the security people from Touch." The fuck was I doing?

"Well, if it's not too late, call and we'll go for coffee. I've got to get out of here."

"I'll call. Wait. You talked to Davis. Did you talk to anyone else?"

"Both the others and Randy Brian again."

"Did anyone ask where you were?"

"All of them." That didn't narrow things down much.

Oh well. "Did you tell anyone?"

"No. You said not to."

"Good girl. That still stands."

We said good-byes and I sat for a few minutes thinking about myself. No good came from it.

Three pass-offs and a redial got me Raleigh Lightstep down helping folks at Central Booking.

"Lightstep."

"Wha'sup, dog?"

Silence.

"Hey, Raleigh. You in there?"

"I can't believe the shit you do. Even when I know you gone do it, I can't believe it. See, I know you call me 'bout somebody and I tell you somethin'. Then, just cause you askin' 'bout him, he very subject to end up dead. Then guess what?"

"What?" I couldn't catch up to the game.

"You call me the fuck back. You call a cop? No. You call me. Why, Sloan? Why you make life so fuckin' hard on the people know you?"

"Am I supposed to know what the fuck you're talking about?"

"Talkin' about. . . ?" A chair squeaked. Raleigh was moving. When he spoke it was supposed to be a whisper. "Stephenson Burry. Stiff, dumb-ass. And his sidekick Billy Joe Radcliff, Ratliff, whatever the fuck it is."

"Whoa. Whoa. Back the fuck up. Stiff and Billy Joe?"

"Dead as the movement, dog." Raleigh paused. "You just now findin' out, ain't you?"

"Just now. How?"

"Two versions floatin' around. Most popular says you take two peckerwoods, add a big piece of crack cocaine. Put it all on a rice grinder and send it down the road, you get two dead peckerwoods."

"What's the unpopular version?"

"Hold on." Offline: "Scott, go down get us some release forms. We up for a busy evenin'." Scott said something and Raleigh said, "Cause I'm askin' you. Thank you." Back to me. "Fuckin' big ears. Other version says they was playin' bumper car with a Lincoln comin' outta Apopka. Course you wouldn't know nothin' 'bout that. I know you wouldn't

I'm gone hang the fuck up and don't you call your ass here no more."

Raleigh carried through on the threat and hung up. I sat there.

I didn't know how I felt. Fucking Cassandra. I keep telling people how they're going to get dead and they don't hear me. I know I should have felt bad for a mother in a discount motel in Fernandina. Not because she and her children had lost something. But because she had to raise two kids on lies about what a piece of shit their father wasn't.

There was something wrong as hell with me. Inside. As hard as I looked for some guilt to drag around, all I could think about was the opportunity that had presented itself to mix business and pleasure this evening. I'd been crawling in mud all day; time to refresh.

I detoured by the fridge, grabbed a Newcastle and sterilized it in the shower for a couple of days. Sterilized myself along with the Newcastle. I felt a little cleaner, and dragging a blade over my not so fresh face made me look a little cleaner. A shot under the arms put me at flipping through my rags. I found a decent shirt with buttons and a pair of jeans new enough they didn't have many secrets yet. The me in the mirror tried ankle boots, kicked them and slid into an old friendly pair of pigskin Borns. A soft, black fine-cord jacket, and I looked like somebody. I was clean, shaved and nearly sober, and I didn't give a shit who knew it.

The message machine was flashing again. I punched the button again. Terry with good news again. "Sloan, if you come in, check the local twenty-four-hour news station."

I punched up channel 13 and got their man on the street. He was standing several yards away from a Cadillac that looked a lot like the one taking a bath in Sammy Bardicello's drive earlier. Offscreen, a head was asking if the police were releasing any info. The head in the street said no but they had talked to a witness. It was quite gruesome and he felt bad about having to report on it. He hid his glee and told us how someone pulled up at a traffic light and fired a shotgun at the driver of the car, killing him instantly.

Wait. Wait a minute. Breaking news and the head back in the studio had the goat carcass, running with it. Reports suggesting the victim was Sam Bardicello, local restaurateur, were being verified. Yes, the police department had verified the victim was Sam Bardicello, local restaurateur. I couldn't believe it. I didn't believe it.

The bastard had balls. Sam Bardicello wasn't any more in that car than Wayne fucking Newton was. I wondered who Sammy had a beef with. Somebody he'd lost trust with. A sacrificial lamb. Now Sammy could go play a decent game of golf without having to wear his Kevlar skivvies. Sammy the fucking Fish owed me another one. That positioned me perfectly, it seemed, to call one in.

"Lemme speak to Sammy."

"Don't you watch the news?" The neo-torcher admin assistant.

"Yeah, but I take it all with a grain of salt. This is Sloan."

"I know who it is. Shall I pass your condolences on?"

"Yeah. Tell Sammy sorry he's dead and I need that beef he and I discussed."

"I'll tell the family you called."

I held the phone until it rang. My hand didn't spasm over it.

"Hey, Sammy."

Low chuckle. "You figured my play, huh, pal?"

"Saw you coming a mile away, daddy. Who was the chump?"

"Guy named Schtenski."

"Ah, the caviar crowd. You solve a problem? I mean besides the obvious."

"Yeah. Fuckin' Cossack. The guy threatenin' *me*. So I give him a nice car, a decent suit of clothes, kiss his cheek, send him on his way."

"That suit of clothes? You wearing it earlier in the day?"

"Maybe, baby. Hey, where'd you get me?"

"Driving your own car? Sammy, sweetheart, you're much too the large shot for such nonsense."

"Oh." He sounded disappointed. "I thought maybe you figured I was smarter than to go get dead."

"That too. You got some mokes I can use this evening, maybe in the morning?"

"Sure thing. You got something in mind?"

"Putting thought to it. Listen, Sammy, I may end up with a couple of peckerwood ridgerunners on my hands. I do, you interested?"

"Whatchu got in mind? And easy on how you put it."

"Maybe you could trade out with their clubhouse. Barter or fish bait, I don't really give a shit. These guys are outta fucking hand."

"I hear you. Yeah. Yeah, I could do somethin'. I do, you owe me."

"No. You do, we're even."

I got some of the little low chuckle. "Nah. I'll still owe you. Just jerkin' your chain a little. You need magillas, you got 'em. Let me get one of 'em on the line, you tell 'em what you want."

"Hey, Sammy, how long you planning on staying dead?"

"Till after tax day if I'm lucky. Let me get that tough-guy for you."

I rang Terry back soon as I could. "Sammy-the-Fish lives."

113

She drew in a sincere breath. "Oh God. Thank God."

"Well, keep in mind, someone had to die to get the network's attention."

"Oh God." Different than before. "Who?"

"Some Russian wiseguy. A guy who kept stepping on people's toes, I hear."

"You don't sound real choked-up about it."

"Welcome to America."

NINETEEN

The garage Sarah Lee had mentioned was between my place and hers. Between my place and the garage I remembered a highbrow boozery. When I pulled up out front I knew I was in the right place. It had applied the extra *p* and *e* to shop and had a trellis with a plastic grapevine in the front window.

An older couple were asking me questions like I was applying for a job, not looking for some advice on upscale sauce. We had talked some about regions and grape skins. We called some of the grapes bastards and looked down our noses at California a bit. I could have done that all evening, but the lady asked me what my expectations were from this bottle of wine, and I said getting laid. She suggested a gallon of Gallo and disappeared into the stockroom.

The man was trying hard not to laugh, I know he was. "You have a date?"

"Yeah. With a very nice lady."

"What are you looking to spend?"

Let's see, I've got fourteen grand. "What'll a hundred bucks do?"

He motioned with his hand. We went to a section with French regions stenciled on the wall over it. I figured I was about to get some more sheep shit on vino horticulture but the old guy put a hand on his mouth and mumbled to himself. He pulled a couple, blew the light coat of dust off, slid them back. He pulled one he liked. "Here." He slapped it in my hands. "Come over here."

We mumbled over some port for a little and he chose again. "Here. You'll need this for after dinner."

"This'll work?"

My man grinned an experienced grin. "Eighty-five bucks on the wine, twenty-six on the port. You don't get laid, you come by later, I'll fuck you."

I caught the grin. A bad case of it. "Guarantee like that, no wonder your grapevine's flourishing."

"We get mostly women customers. Same offer for everyone though."

The guy had a six of Guinness, no Newcastle, no Harp, no Bass. I gave him twelve bucks for it along with the other buck eleven for the good stuff. He wasn't that cute, but at a buck thirty and change after the governor's cut, he better hope I got laid.

An angel in a loose cotton top and loose jeans waved a hand at me. I showed her a palm and parked. Sarah met me halfway with a smile and a couple of grocery bags. I took the bags and opened the Jag's door for her. She slid in and I shoved the bags in a rear door and got in.

"In all fairness, I don't drive a car like this."

Sarah smiled. "I know. I could smell."

I looked across my eyes in her direction. "More, please."

"It's a woman's car. A woman with exquisite taste in perfumes. Is it the prostitute's?"

"Yes."

"And I know what you drive."

"And everything else there is to know?"

She wasn't embarrassed about it. "What there is. You lead a very private life."

"Simple life would be more accurate. There's just not that much to know." Was I actually shooting for modesty?

"Oh, I don't know. There was some very interesting stuff. Just not much of it." Nice smile. "So what did you find out about *me?*"

"Let's see. You're second-level security officer for Touch Ministries. You should make more than you do but the position is more about prestige and résumé, so you drive a four-year-old Bavarian nightmare and live a tad more frugally than you'd like. You're the child of Vietnamese immigrants, a good dose of French tossed in. You were the tallest person in your class until tenth grade. You shoot a mean game of nine-ball and wear a revolver cross-draw on your left hip unless you're casual, in which case, I'd guess you carry it in that big purse there. Your best meal is seafood *panang* and if you're going to sleep with someone, you usually do so on the first date." Whew. "Oh, did I mention you're beautiful?"

I had her laughing with a hand up to her mouth. "Oh God, Duncan. You're a riot. You don't own a computer, do you?"

"Yeah. I own one. We're just not friends. Well?"

"Not bad. Tallest until ninth grade. The *panang* got me."

"I saw chilies, cream and shrimp in your bag."

"Okay. How'd you figure out the first-date thing?"

"I didn't. Just good old-fashioned wishful thinking."

Sarah Lee's house was wooden, tiny and high off the ground. I suspected it was, at one time, an ancillary to one of the massive brick behemoths that turned their backs to her. Cozy. Homey. Nothing fancy. Family pictures, friend pictures. Some nice oriental stuff here and there. Enough to remind you but not burden you. It had a stair that creaked and a fireplace that drew.

I liked it. It was comfortable and it smelled of girl.

117

I moseyed around and looked at pictures and knickknacks while Sarah hid the groceries and prepped her kitchen. I made it back around and asked, "Wine?"

"Sure, whatcha got?"

I showed her and she ooed. Then I showed her that if you give me the corkscrew, you'll get cork in your wine. I gave myself the obligatory dash and held the glass up. "To what?"

Her glass came in my direction. "To truth."

"To truth, then." Glasses clinked.

The Guinness, when I got to it, was old and flat but the ambiance had everything bubbly. I hardy noticed. While Sarah diced and sliced and simmered, I asked, "How does a girl like you end up in a place like this?"

"The house? A friend sold it to me."

"No. The life. Doing security at Holy World. Baby-sitting a charismatic slug?"

"Oh. That place. She gets a master's degree in criminal justice, interns at a law firm, and changes directions."

"Ethics dilemma?"

"Yes. I had some."

"Those ethics feel like orphans over at the law firm?"

"I never got a chance to pull them out."

"Just as well. That way you didn't have to bring them home and scrub them. We're beating hell out of lawyers, aren't we?"

"Yes, but no more than is deserved. What about Duncan Sloan? He used to have a real job. A wife. Two cars, the boat, the whole deal?"

"Yeah. Pretty much."

"So how does a boy like that end up in a place like this?"

Boredom, complacency, fear of complacency? Sloth? "Sense of place. More accurately: loss of."

"Explain, please." Her back was to me, one of her four best sides. "While you peel shrimp."

I stood next to her at the sink and we watched nothing through a dark window.

"I've always been short on a lot of required qualities, but through it all, I always knew who I was. One morning I woke up and didn't recognize anything anymore. A wife lying next to me I didn't know. A house arranged by someone else. A life arranged by someone else. Company car; company man. A highly parametered life." I shrugged. "Mostly I didn't know *me* anymore. I started bucking. I don't know that I've stopped yet."

"No. You haven't stopped." Sarah turned to face me. "You never will. Not again."

"That doesn't exactly sound like it puts me on the most-available list." I stuck my hands under the tap and wiped them with a towel.

She placed the knife in her hand on the cutting board. "No. But it does make you one sexy son of a bitch." She kissed me like she meant every word of it. We did that for a while, my hands gliding over her, feeling good about where life had taken them.

Sarah broke the clench, patted my chest. "Okay, Mr. Sloan, peel the shrimp."

"You started it."

I got a look that could have started a war, would have made a Greek spend the night crouched in a wooden horse. "And I'll finish it."

"I'll hold you to it. Wine?"

The *panang* may have been perfect. The view from my side of the table was. I was trying hard to keep from tossing the food down the chute, grabbing the port and getting along to finishing what Sarah had started. Trying so hard you should

119

have smelled my brakes burning. They may have smelled perfect. Like I say, my mind was busy with other things.

Sarah refrigerated items requiring such and I slammed the dirties in the washer like they were on fire. A hug or two in the kitchen, a serious kiss or two, and we moved on.

The port. A few Van Morrison songs turning us in tight circles in her tiny living room. Some unnecessary articles of clothing falling around. Then it was Sarah Lee and me just how we were set on earth, a single candle flickering, Van easing it down, killing it slowly with some alto sax. Then silence and two bodies tangled to one, standing at the stair. I leaned over, puffed the candle to sleep.

There was nowhere to go but up. Similar creatures, similar habits, we grabbed our handguns and I followed her, a beautiful, sinewy, naked thing with a .357 Mag in her hand, up the stair. I would have followed her out the second-story window if she'd kept walking.

Lucky for me, she stopped at a bed the size of Islamorada. Luckier for me, she knew what to do when she got there. It was nice. It was her; it was caramel and cinnamon.

First there was soft harmony. A tuning. Then right into the finale. The finale was louder and bolder. It exploded, running, flaring like heat lightening.

I skinnied down and got the port and we sat naked on the bed drinking from the bottle until we finished it. Trading stories, learning secrets that hung on to the words, revealing pieces intentionally or accidentally.

It wasn't late but I leaned back against some pillows and closed my eyes. A soft face kissed my chest and snuggled into it. I had found a place to die.

That thought led to a be-careful-what-you-wish-for thing via a couple of hillbilly hit men. I might have dozed; I was a million miles away when the phone rang and it scared the shit out of me. I jumped; Sarah laughed.

She flicked on a lamp and said yes into a handset. I let my face have a good time nuzzling her back while she said yes a few more times, maybe some other stuff, then I heard the one I usually drop on my dates.

"I'll be there in twenty minutes." Hang up.

An exhale brought her around, up on one elbow facing me. "I've got to go."

Her breasts jiggled when she talked. "Something's happened at Rembert's compound. Stop looking at my tits."

"What?"

She looked at me, I looked up from where I was looking. She was balking. "There's been some trouble."

"To truth?"

We had to think about it a bit. "Someone broke in the compound. Shots were fired. No one on our side was hurt, but Ross thinks one of *them* was hit."

"Cowboy hats?"

"I don't know."

I wrinkled my brow. "Why?"

I'd lost cupcake. "Why what?"

"Why the Experience? What does that get anyone?"

Sarah clued in and smiled at me being dumb.

I got it. "You're kidding. The man works, eats, sleeps, shits inside that fence. Goes out for pussy." I got amused thinking about it. The guy *was* a slug.

"And Church's chicken. He loves to go out for Church's chicken. Goes inside, touches the masses."

"They all know who he is?"

"I guess. They act like it. They know he's someone, two-thousand-dollar suit, stretch limo."

"It must be quite moving. Almost mystical, all the Mel-Fry in the air."

"Makes you want to cry."

"Yeah. That Mel-Fry'll do that to you."

I got up. "I'll drive you. Let me get our clothes."

"I don't think so."

I leaned on a door casing. "Ross the boss get mad if you bring in an outsider?"

"It's not just that. He'll want to know why you were here at ten-thirty."

"Tell him I was naked and couldn't leave that way. What do you care what he thinks?"

"Duncan, think about where I work. There's a morality clause in my contract."

I had plenty to say about that but I stood on it. I just said, "Call Ross. Tell him you're bringing me. He'll agree. Trust me."

Sarah was in bra and panties when I got back topside with our duds. Her head came through her shirt and she said, "You were right. He said he needed to talk to you. He'll try to pump you."

"Yeah, but mostly he's interested in spin and discretion. Way it's going, he'll wave some cash at me. Wanna bet?"

She snapped a snap and zipped a zipper as she walked over. I was doing the one-leg balance and she steadied me, up close. "Why would you bet with me? Right now, anything I have is yours."

I put a hand behind her head, pulled her in. "How about double or nothing?"

"You want double, you got double."

TWENTY

Hit a wasp nest with a stick. That was our reception at Touch. Showing in a strange car, Terry's Jag, it took a few different faces looking in the car for even the vice chancellor her-own-self to get though security.

Scene replayed at a second gate, we were in the facility's core where God's own lay his weary head. From the exterior, it was just one of several hunks of concrete and steel with windows stuck around at predictable places. Inside, a hall fit for kings.

Sarah and I trudged through carpet so thick you had to walk on tiptoe to keep it from tickling your ass. Some real art, a tad racier than what was on display for the ticket holders. Objects in glass cases that must have been art simply because they were in glass cases. Tapestries older than a lot of countries hung on twenty-foot-high walls. The lighting was done by Hollywood with the emphasis on the divine.

The only brothers we encountered were of the order of the gun, grim faces moving with purpose, communicating with the silence of ants when they passed. Someone had hit the wasp nest and all stingers were at ready.

A big blond palooka with no expression swung a door open. Sarah and I used it. Looked like we'd found command central. Video screens flickered out scenes from around the compound with an occasional armed soul passing across. A guy with a headset at a console was busy listening and talking, looking at this screen or that. The center of the room was a war table. A buff man of fifty with expensive hair was talking to several sad faces at the table. I didn't know Ross Grace's style, so I didn't know if he was chewing ass or doing business as usual. Watching his act, I figured the chewing was usual biz.

Sarah approached, came in Grace's line of vision. He never missed a word, but glanced at his watch in silent reprimand. Just for fun, he stopped chewing, said, "Not great response time."

Sarah let it zip by, reading a sheet Grace had pushed at her. "You get anything out of the shamus at dinner?"

Ross Grace didn't know the shamus was behind him, over his left shoulder. Sarah's eye's came up to meet mine. I got to see her blush. I got a good look at her. She didn't look perfect anymore.

"No, but another half hour, I'd have been singing louder than Ethel Merman."

Grace spun and I got to see his stern face. Showboat. Expensive hair, expensive teeth, clean shaven at eleven in the evening. A chin that could have plowed. A long angular nose fucked up the package some, pulling his eyes a tad too close and giving them an almost surprised look.

"Don't you know how to announce yourself, sir?" The sir didn't sound like it was coming from respect.

I made a trumpet with my hand and gave him a little dat-duh-da-dat, saluted like a World War I limey, said, "Private Sloan reporting for duty. Sir." Maybe it was the port. I don't ordinarily drink port.

We squared off mentally, me wondering why I do shit like that, him wondering how you deal with such irreverence. And save face. I could sit on my question but we had an audience. He had to play a card. Queen.

"I can't believe you brought him into the high-security area. That's a direct breech of security, ma'am." He brought out a long finger that had some money invested in the nail. He pointed it at Sarah. "We're under articles here. We're at alpha one alert."

He and the finger had more but I jumped in. "Hey, hey. This is just pretend here. Everything on this end of town is. This isn't a real war. You're not under attack."

"I beg to differ. We were attacked. We remain under attack until I say we're not."

Before the guy fell on the floor and started drumming his fists and heels, I swung the boom and changed tack.

"A couple of guys broke in here. Big deal. Nobody on your team lost any juice over it. Congratulate yourselves. The system held, you ran them off. Everybody did their jobs and the system had a successful test. A helluva test. These guys are specialists, some of the best stuff available. You kicked their butts, put them in the street. Break out the bottled water, have a toast." I took a dramatic look at the faces around the room. "Come on, people. It worked. Give the man a hand."

His peeps gave him a semi-enthusiastic round and he sucked the moment. I pulled up a chair, close in to him, as the soldiers went about their war. "I saved your face right then because you needed it. These gate-crashers aren't above coming back, and I don't wanna feel guilty about fucking up morale around here and what might happen. But don't you ever again attempt to draft me into this fascist Swiss Guard you've built. I don't like you or this place. I hardly know your boss and I already don't like him. You and I have a small bit of business to discuss and that's all, pal. And next time you manage to get a foot in your mouth all by yourself, try and get it out the same way. The troops might respect you a little more."

He didn't like it. "I've got respect, mister."

"No, you don't. You've got some intimidation, but you don't have any loyalty or respect. You did? Somebody in this room would have been on me when I first opened my mouth. They just sat on smiles. You wanna have a beautiful machine? Quit pushing spit shine and procedure. Lead, don't bitch. These people wanted to be in the army, they'd go join the fucking army. You wanna be in the army, re-up."

No one but Sarah was watching and I was speaking low enough I'm not sure she was getting it all. Grace relaxed his face a little. "You've given that speech before, haven't you?"

"Yeah." A few times.

"When you were with Pepe Costa's outfit?"

"Yes." My ex-pa-in-law. "You know Pepe?"

"Yes. I interviewed with Costa Security when I came out of the Army. Twelve years ago or so. He didn't hire me. He said his son-in-law had threatened to quit if he hired another ex-military. That would have been you? Head of investigative services."

I nodded. "Yeah. We had a rash of ex-military for a run there."

"Did they all hear that edict?"

"Most. Eventually."

"Then considering the quality of what Costa Security is turning out, I'll accept it prima facie as damned good advice. And the shamus comment was from Pepe. I called him today. Of course you know we ran you."

"Of course." I looked at Sarah. She should have been having a better time, but her face looked like the world had shifted a little, catching her in a cramped place she didn't want to be.

"He gave you rave praise. I didn't pass that on to Ms. Lee, and I should have. It was Pepe who came up with shamus."

"Was it meant as a compliment?" I knew Pepe and respected him. I also knew him well enough to know any compliment from him could have a back edge to it. That seemed to be the case.

"Well, I'm sure. He was complimenting your free spirit. Your lone-wolf image."

Jeez. I might puke the carpet. "Probably more the lone-wolf thing. Listen. I look around and don't see any cops. Am I to assume you're going to let what happens at home stay at home?" I gave him a few, added, "Considering the tree all this sprouts from."

He showed me how he wasn't a quick thinker for a bit. Then: "I guess to a large degree that depends on you. What are your views on police involvement in this *situation?*" The way he said the last word it might have had a maggot on it.

"Very dim. I need a day or two to cap this thing off. I think. If things go to plan. This crap, like what went on tonight, should stop. I figure it'll take the money behind this situation a few days to regroup and find new talent. All goes well, I give the cops the bad guy, they chew on my ass for two or three hours, I go home and no one says squat about anybody else."

"You said they could come back tonight."

I shrugged. "You never know. Keep the manpower on site, keep them moving. If one of your visitors was hurt, I'd bet on them calling it a night."

"We definitely hit one of them. We had small traces of blood on a wall, a few drops on a sidewalk."

"No. Listen to me. You didn't hit one of them. He probably cut himself. No one here shot anyone. Right?"

Ross Grace was pretty but not brilliant. That probably had more to do with Pepe not hiring him than my opinions. Pepe pretty much hired and fired who the fuck he wanted. Ross finally got what I was saying.

"Okay. Yes. No. No one shot anybody, so no one has to file

a firearms report or anything. Right. Just a couple of intruders. Our team confronted them. Parties stood down."

"Perfect. I'll keep you people posted." Then to Sarah, "You need a ride?"

She looked at Grace and he at her, nothing passing that I saw, but she said, "I'm going with you. Is that okay, Ross? I'll relieve you at seven."

"Yes. That's fine, Sarah. It was an honor meeting Pepe Costa's son-in-law."

"Ex-son-in-law. The shamus." I made a hand pistol at him and he mimicked it.

The parking lot was quiet, as was the interstate. As was the ride back to the cupcake's place. I missed her street and circled around to the drive. We took the little brick walk to the steps and I looked at the sky, said good night, smiled nice and turned, using the walk.

"Goddam it, Duncan."

I stopped but didn't turn. "Goddam what?"

A few frustrated seconds. I really know how to handle women. I really know how to piss them off. "Just goddam it. Goddam everything. Goddam you."

I half turned. "Goddam me?" I let the stars shine on my palms.

"You. For being so goddam perfect. Too goddam perfect to be part of the world. Too goddam perfect to give someone a chance to say they're sorry. Too tall and straight and perfect."

"Well, don't grow up to be perfect like me, cupcake. You wanna be tall and straight, weather the storm, you gotta cut all the limbs off. Then you're not a tree anymore. You're just a lightening rod stuck in the ground. You sit up there just waiting for it. Like you want it to happen."

"Then why do you do it?"

I stretched my mouth flat, shrugged. "Hell if I know."

"You've got to let me explain, apologize."

"For what?"

"For not telling you Ross expected me to pump you."

"Oh that. I didn't know what you'd done, the way your face has been drooping. Jesus, cupcake, I know that. I can't say I came here with only one motive myself. It was the most motivating motive, but not a lone-wolf motive." I turned completely; I faced her. "You just got caught."

"So what was all this?"

"All what? I'm just grabbing my smokes."

"You said good night."

"Has been for me. How about you?" I was smiling but just barely.

She started to speak a couple of times before it took. "You bastard." She shook her head, tilted it, hands on hips. Nice slim hips. "You are the most exasperating, asinine son of a bitch I've ever seen in my life."

"Yeah?"

"Yeah. And you think this is all too damn funny, don't you? You fucking shamus." The flush in her face was conceding to a randy smile.

"Takes one to know one."

"Yeah? Wanna spend the night, shamus?"

"Only if I can follow you upstairs."

"And what will I be wearing?"

"I gotta say, you didn't look bad with just the three-fifty-seven. What was it, a Ruger?"

"Mmm-hmm."

"Go with the Ruger, then."

We used the steps, then Sarah used a key and stepped back, allowing me to be chivalrous. I grasped the opportunity and swung the door open.

Then I neutralized it. "Whatcha gonna tell Ross when he asks if I took the money?"

The cupcake was crossing in front of me, breasts brushing my chest, face down. I don't know what I expected but I didn't get it when her smiling face turned up.

What I got? "I'll tell him it turns out you're not that sort of boy."

I locked the door; Sarah made the first stair.

"How much?"

She turned. "Five for keeping us up to date. Five to twenty for discretion."

"Maybe I *am* that sort of boy." I was at the stair.

Sarah, taller than me on the step, put her arms around my neck, kissed me nicely. "No you aren't. You like to tell yourself you are, but when it comes down to it, you aren't."

"You get that off your computer?"

"No. I got that lying on my back looking up at your face."

The hell do you say? I just pointed up the stair, slapped her on the ass when she turned.

TWENTY-ONE

Six? Maybe earlier. Not good light out yet. I cracked an eye and saw Sarah coming back into the bedroom. Blouse, makeup, hairdo, bagel. No pants. I'm always amazed at the asexual way women approach nudity. Men get naked from the waist down, we're thinking about something, while women go about nonchalantly, bagel in hand. Half clothed, half naked. It's all in the outlook.

I closed the eye and said, "Wanna even up?"

"Who owes who what?"

"You owe me. For getting caught." I raised my head and dragged another pillow under it, blinked my eyes open. The flag below the blouse hem waved at me.

Sarah had her arms crossed, bagel out, away from the blouse. "Up here, pal."

My eyes were reluctant. I didn't blame them for grumbling when they had to move up.

"I thought we put that behind us."

"One question. From truth. I look around the room at Touch and I don't see but one person with the panache to pull off this pruning of the list. So one question. From truth. Are you doing it?"

From her face I didn't know if I'd insulted her or complimented her.

"I thought you meant Ross."

"Hell no." I answered like she had asked if Gil Scott-Heron was a pacifist.

"Or Rembert."

"I haven't met His Holiness, but I'm taking your word on that. I've caught his act on TV and I don't see it either." Now we could get around to her.

There was a funny near smile on her face. "You think I could do something like this?"

"Could? Yeah. In the sense of having the brains and the balls. Sure. Are you smart enough to toss up a herring like getting some guys to break in? Sure."

I got up, walked over to her. I flipped her hair across one eye like a gun moll. "The *would* you part? I don't know, but I'm looking forward to getting to know you that well."

The sentiment got me a nice full body hug and some cream cheese on the back. Sarah held on for a while. I held on too. But I didn't forget she hadn't answered the question.

Please don't make me ask again.

From down in my neck area a muffled voice said, "I would never be a part of anything like that."

"That's what I thought, cupcake. I just had to hear it."

We broke the clench and I stepped in yesterday's clothes and gun. I dropped the clip, checked it good, reracked it. "I'm going for a walk."

From the bathroom: "Where?"

"A walk. Around the block."

"I'm leaving soon."

"You're gone when I get back, I'll leave too."

Sarah stepped out, tiny brush in fingers. "What are you doing?"

"I wanna make sure the hitters aren't in the bushes."

I got a flat stare. "Why would they be?"

I smiled nice. "Because I'm next."

She was processing. "Why?"

"Ninety-five percent sure thing, I got next to the right guy yesterday. Doing so, I moved into prime position."

Quizzical look. "What about our place last night? The break-in?"

"I figure that was already in the oven. Planned and plotted. I bet, you look at security tapes a day or so back, you'd see a couple guys could be Baptist deacons checking you out."

"So you set this up for here?" She wasn't so happy anymore.

"No. Last night was done. And if not, what better place could I have been? Somebody like you watching my back."

"And your front. You think they're out there?"

I shrugged out genuine ignorance. "They'll pick me up somewhere today, follow my sign for a bit. Who knows? I'm gonna go see."

"And if they are?"

"I'll come back first. Wanna go play with them? You'd be late for guard duty."

I got a nice grin over a head shake. "I'll call it work."

"Call it what you will, just don't call Ross and tell him." Her face prompted me. "No use confusing him. He's had a rough night."

"And you don't trust him?"

"I don't trust *myself* half the time, cupcake."

A Florida fog fuzzed up the streetlights and amplified the sounds of my feet on the sidewalk. I moved along with purpose, trying to act like I belonged here. There were some highbrow, white-bread mothers in this little cut, guys that know how to call a cop, and I didn't need cops. There were few spots a car could sit semi-unnoticed, I'd make it fast.

Last night when I missed Sarah's drive it wasn't an accident. My personal favorite semi-secluded spot was the favorite of the 'Bama boys too. A copse of Australian Pines was in an imperialistic mood near the south of the little park across the way, gobbling up ground like it was invited to the party. They don't get called invasive exotics for nothing.

It actually surprised me when I glimpsed the car's grill peeking out of the trees. After last night, with Cecil and Ray Gene being out after the chickens had racked and one of them needing some gauze and adhesive tape, I wasn't expecting it. I was okay the way it was playing though.

On the hike back around the long way to Sarah's I called the head magilla Sammy had lent me. I was surprised to find him awake and told him about it.

"Hey, you don't call last night? I know we're on for this mornin'. You ain't dealin' wit' just another pretty face here."

"You always wake up in love with yourself, Tony?"

"Yeah. How we playin' this?"

"Know where Delaney Park is?"

"Yeah. I been to town a couple o' times. Nice area. Should I put on fresh panties?"

"Nah. Just shave your knuckles and grab a couple of large automobiles and a few of your clones. You get close, give me a call. I'll guide you through the parts where you have to think."

"Hey. Sloan. You look up and I ain't there, write it off to the smart mouth."

"You hang up, call somebody who owes you money. They'll act like they believe you. See you quick as you show."

Four stairs had me on Sarah's back porch. I closed the door, said, "We're on if you're game."

She was game. Dark T-shirt. She had painted on a pair of dark jeans. Black sneakers. *No* .357—a Browning High Power was in a sling crossing from shoulders to rest under her breasts.

134

A black suede coat hid the gat when she fastened the middle button.

She reached behind her, grabbed her hair, and twisted and pinned until it stuck out behind like grouse feathers.

"Ready?" She was.

"Soon. I'm waiting on a couple of tanks for ground support. Coffee would be a good thing."

I perched on a low stool with Sarah across from me. The coffee did me good. I was becoming human. We drifted off business at hand some, chatting about things that didn't matter much. The ruse was as thin and unconvincing as an undertaker's smile. The talk slowly exploded into silence.

"How does this go?" Sarah's eyes came from the surface of her coffee to me when she said it.

"We box them in. You and I step in, take control."

"What if they start shooting?"

"Shoot back."

"Then what?"

My mouth was in motion when my cell played my song, saved me from looking unprepared.

"Yeah?"

"Hey. We're in the hood." Tony "The Sneer."

"See the little park."

Hesitation. "Yeah, we got it."

"See the Australian pines on the south?"

"Which way's south, pal?"

Toward Miami, musclehead. "You came in from the east. Left is south."

"These pine trees, they like big motherfuckers? Like giant Christmas trees?"

"You got it, Tony. See the Lincoln setting in there?"

"I see a car. Could be a Lincoln, could be a fuckin' Edsel."

"Whatever, you see us walking across the park, you do the

thing. Bump them, you want to, let them know we're coming in strong."

"You got it. We gonna pop these guys?"

"Not unless they want us to. Anybody drops a cap, you do what you feel like."

"Your call. Sammy says whatever you say. You want 'em popped, we pop 'em. Otherwise we take 'em back to talk wit' Sammy."

I didn't ask; I didn't care. "You take them."

"My pleasure. When you comin'?"

"Right now. Gimme three minutes and start your move."

"See you at the party."

TWENTY-TWO

The walk, three hundred yards or so, was brisk. Keep moving. Hope nobody's outside the car taking a piss or anything. A hundred yards: put your hand on your piece. Fifty: break it out, throw the safety off. Twenty yards: split off. We're in the trees now. Where the fuck's Tony and his crew?

The hats were relaxed, slumped down. Honky-tonk seeped out closed windows. I went down and skittered across the path behind the car, into the trees again, now on the driver's side. Then car sounds, then headlights, funny-colored in the young light of a new day, swinging in from each direction.

The twin Caddies boxed the Lincoln, Tony coming on in to rap the cowboys pretty good from behind. I stepped from the trees, slightly behind the driver's door, noted Sarah's position and made costume jewelry out of the plate glass window by Ray Gene's head with my piece.

"Goddam, son." His hands went up to plain view.

"Cecil, in case you hadn't noticed, there's a little girl over there with a big-ass Browning pistol."

"Uh-huh. I see her. She looks like she wouldn't mind shootin' a fella."

"Keep thinking that thought while we count four hands on the dashboard." I counted four, reached in and unlocked the doors.

Over the car, I said, "Keep that Browning right where it is. Anybody much as hiccups, you kill Cecil."

The car smelled like Old Spice and alcohol. Isopropyl. There were some small boxes with crosses on them scattered on the backseat. Gauze and tape.

I slid in and put the serious end of my gun in Ray Gene's neck. "Who got winged?"

Ray Gene motioned with his head. "Cecil."

So far, they hadn't figured this out. Here I was. There they were. There was the girl from the holy park. And the guys milling around with shotguns and full auto shit were making even me nervous.

"You all right, Cecil?"

"Yeah. Nothin' but a scratch. What we doin' here?"

"Depends on you and Ray Gene. You think you got a play, you're gonna get dead in the next little bit. You mind your manners, take a ride with these guys, talk to their boss, who knows? Maybe you can work something out. Not my problem."

Cecil didn't really like asking. "Who's their boss?"

"The guy in the Cadillac you blasted? It wasn't him. His car, his clothes. Not him, though."

Cecil's head shook a little. "Ah fuck. What are they? Eyetalians?"

"Like pizza, my man. You're in the wrong fucking town, friends. The girl? Her boss is the preacher. See how it stacks up? You got people all over you. Take the ride, call Phoenix City, work something out."

Tony was coming up, opening Ray Gene's door. "Let's go, Jethro. Easy does it, hands out like a fairy."

Ray Gene shook his head, said, "Shit, Cecil, this ain't gone be a fun mornin'."

A young guy with an eighth inch of hair and an earring dehardwared Ray Gene, patting him down good. They walked him back to the Caddy behind the Lincoln and put him in the passenger front.

I slid out as Tony excused himself to Sarah. She hadn't got it yet. She moved and Tony got Cecil out so the buzz cut could feel him up.

Over the car, she said, "What's happening?"

I had dreaded walking across the open ground of the park. I always dread that break-point moment when you take someone. I shudder to think what could have gone down if a cop happened by. All of that, and I think we were at the part I had dreaded most. "They're going with Tony."

"Cut the shit, Sloan. Going where with Tony?"

She wanted to hear me say: Cop house. I said, "To talk to Sam Bardicello."

"I don't think so." She was coming around the car. "What happens when they talk to the godfather?"

Tony jumped in. "Easy on the godfather stuff, lady." Looking at me like I needed to handle the missus.

I thought Sarah was going to shoot him. I jumped in. "Hey, Tony, how about you give us a couple of minutes here?"

"Sure." He's still standing there.

"Alone would be good."

"Oh. Hey, yeah. I been married three times. What I don't know about women, huh? Take your time."

"Thanks, Tony." He didn't know this one. Neither did I.

Tony walked Cecil to the front Caddy, talking to the crew now. I took a deep breath, looked off at the horizon.

"There's an old saying, not related to the present case other than coincidentally. It goes: You want justice, go to the whorehouse; you wanna get fucked, go to the courthouse." I tossed in a pause. "I don't know what happens when they have their meet with Sammy. I don't give a shit. I know what

139

happens if I take them to the courthouse. So do you. Fifty-fifty, nothing. Everybody clams; everybody walks. Otherwise, they talk a little, get six years state time, do two. So whatchu got? Six dead, and these guys get, like, four months per episode? And sure, the dead people are whoremongers at best, crackheads, thieves and thugs at worst. But they're part of my goddam ecosystem. They wanna maim and kill each other, fine. No outsiders allowed to participate."

The face I was getting, I couldn't tell if she was amused or overwhelmed by my street politics. I didn't think she was amused. She wasn't.

I got a couple of sarcastic laughs that were more like coughs. "Judge Sloan. Jurist Sloan. Executioner Sloan." Dragging the "Sloan" out for days. "I love this." She shook her head, put the gat back in the basket, buttoned her coat. "You're a sociopath. That's what you are. A classic fucking sociopath."

"But I'm blithe. And I'm no executioner."

"What's the difference? You give them to the spaghetti club?"

I shrugged and held it while I said, "Sammy may let them go. They cut a deal." I dropped the shrug.

The cupcake's hands were out and she had a why-me expression going, spinning on her heels to face away from me. She shook her head and crossed her arms. "What happens if he lets them go?"

"They're through here. They're outta the sportsmens' club back home. You drop a job, you don't get another chance, where they live."

I was expecting to be asked what if Sammy took the ridge runners on one of his family fishing trips. I wasn't. She just said, "So you're okay with this, the way it played out?"

"No, I'm not okay with it, cupcake. I just keep thinking about six guys that got dead."

140

Her back was still to me and I could see her head nodding.
"I'm going back to the house."
"See you in a few."
"I'll be gone."
You're already gone, baby.

TWENTY-THREE

Now, goddammit, I had a couple of days to pinch this thing off. I was ready. All except for the slightest idea of how to play out from here. And I had to play out before new talent showed up. I was up to my eyes with dead guys and looking forward to a break. Look hard, Sloan.

A shower and a change of clothes sent me north from town. I scrolled up Terry's cell number, punched redial.

"So you didn't run out on me."

"Hardly. Been working straight through since we talked." In a very general, loose sense, I had been.

"Sure you have, *mon petit chou.*"

"Late breakfast interest you?"

"Intensely."

"What's close?"

"My place."

"What should I bring besides your car?"

"An appetite."

Eggs Benedict made with Nova and onion. Mimosas. Cheese grits. Sesame *dim sum.* Cuban coffee. A breakfast about Florida's mélange.

It was ten-thirty after an early and busy morning. I damaged the layout. Damaged myself. It was so enjoyable it probably took two years off my life.

While we ate, I told her about talking to Sammy about

142

being dead. The Russian. How that got done. The break-in at Rembert's. I left out the part about going out there with Sarah, then spending the night at her place.

I told her about the red-dirt cowboys. She wasn't any more thrilled with the outcome than Sarah, but put up no sentiment. She showed me her discomfort with the eyes. They were the deep green of a forest.

"This security person, is she a woman?" That's all she asked when I was done.

"Yes." I let it drop. It was quiet like a bag of pot lids. "You know everything I've got is pointing at Davis Cambridge?"

A few moments, then, "Yes."

I nodded. "Think about this very carefully. Is there any reason other than embarrassment that might make a successful attorney kill enough guys to make up a basketball team?"

"No. And I've thought about it, Sloan. Maybe there's something in his past." I got a nice shrug with it.

"Maybe it's not about him. Maybe it's about you." I let that float out there. "Maybe there's something in your past. Bright ideas in that direction? Family secrets to share?"

I couldn't see her face. It was down, looking at the tabletop. I don't think I wanted to see it. She was about to lie to me.

"No."

I used my boardinghouse reach and a finger under the chin to lift her head. "Red, talk to me here."

The head was up but now the eyes were closed. She was a creamy dream. Her lids flickered but no tears came.

"The Sebrings are about nothing *but* secrets, Sloan." The eyes opened and she found my hand where it was on the table. "I can't say it. You'll find out. Don't make me say it." Nearly mechanical. Creepy-toned.

I squeezed the hand. "That's fine. I just want you to know

I'm going in there. I can't stop it now, Terry. Where it goes, I go. But I wanna be sure you see it coming."

I got a quick nod and she rose and left the table. I began clearing dishes and debris from our breakfast. I tossed the used dishes in the dishwasher and was looking for leftover containers when she came back in.

"Thank you. You're great, Sloan." She was composed, rigid. A plastic version of herself.

"Yeah. I'm great. Could I hold you for a minute?"

Terry Sebring took up the invitation and held on to me like I was the last breath of fresh air in town. I thought she'd cry, get it out and fuck up the front of my shirt. She never made a peep. We stood there like that for a very long time.

The clench broke with a pat to my chest and, "You're something else, Sloan." I got something new from the green eyes. "You're a hundred different people, aren't you?"

"Aren't you?" Aren't most of us?

Terry did the Zen breath thing I'd seen before. "Okay. Enough of that. What are we going to do about Davis Cambridge?"

"Draw him out into the sunlight."

"How do you do that?"

"I don't have the foggiest notion. I was hoping you did. Let's sit down, finish the coffee, figure something out."

Terry grabbed fresh cups and the hot carafe and we took our designated places at the table.

"I don't know much about Davis, really. He's not a regular. He's a call-when-he's-coming client. I've had him do some property law for me, but not much. Besides that, he works a great deal, according to him. And as I told you, his wife is bedridden. Infirm, as he refers to it. I understand he leads a lonely home life."

I nancied my coffee up and thought out loud. "If he knows

the 'Bama boys are off the job, he's just finding out. The finesse here lies in playing a card while he's between shooters. If he grabs something quick and local, it'll be ugly and incompetent. He'd have exposure like a mother. They'd be scooter bums from Daytona or thug lifers from the hood. Maybe *hermanos* from Brown Tar Alley. That's our local selection." Her expression earned her a "What?"

Terry's eyes were sparkling. "Just amazed at what you do to make a living. The things you have to think about, the people you have to know. And coming from me, that's saying a mouthful."

"There's not a lot of difference in what you and I do, Terry. You get to deal with a slightly better crowd, and I generally get to keep my dainties on."

I got a nice laugh. "Enough already. Tell me how we finesse Davis Cambridge."

"We don't know what he's holding as his motivation card. That's his big card. We do know where he's vulnerable. We play to that."

"Sounds like good strategy. How do you apply it?"

"Cambridge has shown us he would go to great lengths to keep this quiet. That's his flinch point. He needs to think I suspect him and that I intend on going to the police."

"Won't he try to pay you off?"

"He won't put much effort to it. We're pretty much past that point in our relationship. I wanna see where he goes after we talk. Who he sees."

"You think other people are involved?" So did she.

"Uh-huh. There's got to be. I need to look at his past and his present. I'll spend some time microfiching at the downtown library today."

"That sounds like fun." She said it like it sounded like torture.

"It's not so bad. Staying on task's the trick with that. You see something from thirty years ago, an ad even, and you're reading it."

"There's another one of your many sides: The Library Sloan. Well . . . get out of here. I've got work to do, too. I've got a big pile of futures I've got to unload before the bell."

"And I've gotta go tell a guy I'm gonna expose his darkest secret. I wish I knew what it was." I found a lot of air and let it out. "Terry, I got a problem: I got a twenty-one-, twenty-two-year-old girl in Fernandina at what she calls Hampton's Inn. She's got a six-year-old and a four-year-old with her. I've gotta figure out how to tell her that her husband's dead. Billy Joe Ratliff. One of the winners who glommed your car."

"He's dead?"

"Uh-huh."

"The other one?"

"Yeah."

"How?"

"They fell off a motorcycle going really fast." Her face prompted me. "Who knows? I looked at the Dixie boys' car. It didn't have any bump marks on it."

She processed. "I'll go up there and tell her. I'm not going to tell her on the phone. What's her name?"

"Rachel. I love you for this. She may need a lift back this way. God, thank you." A ton was off me. I'd rather dodge bullets blindfolded than do shit like that.

TWENTY-FOUR

The way Davis Cambridge and I had hit it off, I didn't see why I should need an appointment. It was a tad before noon. I popped in like poor relations.

The same plywood was at the same trendy angles. The pictures were still in the frames. No one was still visible in the waiting room.

Now that I knew where the door was, I could spot it but it had no knob on my side. I thought maybe a loud rap or two might work. It did.

The suspenders from yesterday opened the door, looked me over like he'd never seen me, said, "Can I help you?" Something in his voice didn't make me think he really wanted to.

"I need to see Mr. Cambridge. Right away."

"I'm sorry. Mr. Cambridge has gone home for the day."

I shook my head slowly for him, emphasizing. "Junior, if you're lying, your boss is going to be very upset with you."

We looked at each other a bit and he said, "He's not here."

"Can you call him for me?"

"No. I've tried several times. He's not answering his cell phone."

He knew something.

"He have a bad morning?"

"Yes."

"You people get a visit from some good ol' boys, white straw cowboy hats, plastic suits?"

147

The suspenders eyeballed me. Finally: "Yes."

"They come by yesterday after I left?"

Again, he had to think hard about it. "Yes, Mr. Bonefy. Several of us here would like to know what's going on." What he meant was several of them would like to distance themselves from the wounded.

"So would I. For different reasons." I gave him one of my more professional smiles. "Polish your résumé up, Junior. You'll be needing it real soon. You talk to him, tell him I said I have to go to the po-leece about he-knows-what." I had a wink but I saved it.

The effort earned me a smile. "Thanks. His house is over by the country club." How quickly loyalty fades.

"I know. You think he's there?"

"His maid says not. Who knows? Are you going over there?"

"I imagine."

"If he's there, would you ask him to call in? The competition won a change of venue in the Breem case."

I laughed. "Trust me, the Breem case is way down on his list of things to worry about."

"So we're through here?" His face was as ambivalent as the question. I could have taken it a couple of ways.

Either way, same answer. "Yeah."

The door closed and became just another fancy plywood panel, and I got out of there. I think I could hear lots being cast in the back room as I left.

Davis Cambridge lived in a sprawl of Florida ranch house backed up to the Country Club of Orlando. It was a short jump and two jogs from downtown, and I was admiring his shrubbery a few minutes later. He had some nice greenery.

There was a circular drive no one else was using, so I did. A simple concrete walk dodged flora to an almost elegant door with lots of glass. I used a buzzer and could hear it fussing through the door.

Someone who could have passed for a maid materialized on the other side of the beveled glass. She had a pleasant face she was bringing in my direction.

The door swung in and I got: "Hello."

My turn. "Hi. Is Mr. Cambridge in?"

I don't know what she thought I was, but I had fooled her. "No he isn't. May I tell him who came by?"

A voice preceded a lady in gardening clothes. "Evelyn, is that the contractor?" Old Florida. The second *e* in Evelyn was tossed out with the *r* on the end of contractor. She stopped and looked me over good. She knew I wasn't a contractor.

"No, ma'am. He's looking for Mr. Cambridge."

"May I help you? I'm his wife."

The lady was late fifties, maybe sixty. Handsome, bold face. Blue eyes that were young. Sun-streaked blond hair with a graceful touch of gray. She wore a denim tunic over a T-shirt and I could see where she had kneeled on the front of the tunic while gardening. Nothing about her seemed infirm in the least.

"I need to see him rather urgently about a client of his. I've got to involve the police and he needs to know." You're at the ocean, why not toss out the hook?

The amused look began to dissipate. "Evelyn, I'll talk to the gentleman," dismissing the maid.

"Yes, ma'am." Evelyn turned and was gone.

"Come in. I've got you standing out on the stoop."

The house was a museum. The furniture, the rugs, the accoutrements, all museum pieces. I was afraid to sit on any of it so I stood.

Mrs. Cambridge sat on a hassock by the fireplace, tucking the loose smock around her legs. "I'm a little confused. I

149

don't know who you are, and Davis's work has never required the police."

I led with a piece of the truth, then stretched it from there. "My name is Sloan. I'm a private investigator. A common client has run into some big trouble and is in danger. I've got to go forward with what I'm sitting on, and what your husband knows about it could place him in an uncomfortable position."

Wisdom was coming from the eyes. "What's this client's name, Mr. Sloan?"

"Sebring." That bought me a peek at something.

"Horace or Sherman?"

"Excuse me?" Maybe I was still fishing a little.

Something happened. Something clicked. "Oh. I see." We gave it a beat. "It's about the girl, isn't it?"

"Which girl is that, Mrs. Cambridge?" Just making sure we were on the same page.

We were. "The Sebring girl. Theresa?"

"Yes, ma'am."

"Is my husband in trouble, Mr. Sloan?"

I didn't have to think about it. "Yes, ma'am. He is."

"Is he going to jail?"

I didn't need time to think, but I put it off for a beat. "I'm afraid so, Mrs. Cambridge."

"Thank you for being candid. I think I had sensed things having gotten out of hand. Davis—Mr. Cambridge—has been in turmoil for days. I asked him more than once what was upsetting him. He came in late again last night and I asked again. He said something about keeping the dead buried. I took it to mean someone who had died long ago. Is this what he was referring to?"

"I'm not sure. Honestly. I don't know what's going on. Mr. Cambridge knows the Sebring brothers?"

"Oh yes. He grew up in Davenport. They went to school

together. He still represents their land interests. They're his biggest clients. Davis sees them at least once a month, I'm sure."

"He been out there lately that you know of?"

The curtain came down. Show over. "Mr. Sloan, I don't think I'd better talk to you anymore. Being an attorney's wife, I have lots of friends who are lawyers. I think I'll go in and call one now."

"Your husband will need a good lawyer." To beat Old Sparky.

"I'm sure he will. No, Mr. Sloan, this is for me. Damage control. Self-defense. Survival. Call it what you want. I've invested thirty-five years in this arrangement. I've put up with condescension, abusive language, infidelity, and yes, an occasional slap across my impertinent mouth. At this juncture, I don't give a fuck what happens to Davis Cambridge the Third. Excuse my French, and excuse me. I have some assets to hide."

"You don't have any idea where he could be?"

"A bar, a golf course, some cheap trick's boudoir. I never know where he is." She smiled like we'd finished our tea and crumpets and it was beddy-bye time. "If you untangle it, you aren't going to believe it. I don't know it all, but what I know is absolutely unfathomable." I got a smile from out around Lake Placid, Okeechobee, somewhere down in that neck of the woods. "My Granddaddy used to say: You're about to jump in the outhouse hole. Jump on in, Mr. Sloan. You may never get clean again. Excuse me."

Then I was alone in the museum. I knew where the door was and I knew how to use it.

I should have wished her good luck with those assets. I agreed with her. Thirty-five years with a rat bastard like Cambridge, she'd earned it.

TWENTY-FIVE

In the outhouse, standing on the seat, contemplating the hole. That would have been Granddaddy Cambridge's version. And, as figurative as it was, I could already smell shit.

The literal life had me in the public library. The Sebrings and Cambridges both went to the beginning of kept records. Nothing too interesting back then. So-and-so marries so-and-so. A property dispute or two. A cousin-on-cousin shooting involving a dog. A poacher shot and killed in the forties. Stuff like that. Then about '64 some stuff about a couple of huge land deals brokered to some dizzy guys from California with big imaginations and even bigger wallets. The unscooped reporters guessing at amounts.

I searched Sebring and Cambridge as a pair and scored. Nineteen sixty-seven. A classic example of Florida true crime qualifying as noir.

It had it all. Convertible T-Birds, booze parties, skinny-dips, flagrant swapping and recoupling. The now-anachronistic word tranquilizers tossed in liberally. Weekend rendez-vous in exciting places like Ormond Beach, Port Charlotte, Jacksonville, Saint Simon's. Fistfights and suicide attempts. Looked like no one had bothered to tell these folks that the swinger era was dead as bobby socks. They had stumbled across the tail end of it and were embracing the passé as only those on the edge of the empire can.

A bunch of cool, swinging heads living in the middle of

nowhere watching their world dissolve before their eyes. The not-a-war in Asia was coming of age and making more and more noise. The Beatles and the Stones had buried the Beach Boys beside Wilson Pickett and Bobby Vinton and Nat King Cole. Funny-looking people were coagulating in places like New York, San Francisco, L.A., but you could see them as far south as Atlanta now, down around Fourteenth and Peachtree. Fuck tranquilizers; these new people were looking for Jamaican collie and LSD-25. Atlas was shrugging. Hold on, swingers.

One of the high priorities of the idle rich youth then, as it's been since the draft was invented, was dodging the draft. College worked. For a while. So did being married. Then Congress ran out of cannon fodder and pulled the deferments. If a guy wasn't smart enough for college or had finished college, the reserves were nice. Lots of guys took the six-year dodge. Weekend warriors. This thing in Southeast Asia would never get big enough to need reservists, right? Right.

Sherman Sebring signed on as a weekend warrior. He got in early one weekend and was having a few drinks with an alibi while his older brother, Horace, was finding Sherman's wife, Jacqueline, dead at the house. Looked like a break-in and burglary gone wrong. The lady of the house was doped on Nembutal, woke up, the guy shot her. The Sebrings' infant daughter, Theresa, was home at the time but slept through the bad parts.

The alibi was a young lawyer named Davis Cambridge. He had run across Sherman at the filling station as he was getting back from bivouacking with Uncle Sam.

Open-and-shut case like this, it seemed Sherman Sebring wouldn't have needed an alibi. It could have been in the conflicting records on time of death. How Jacqueline was shot with a .355-diameter slug which would work in Sherman's

9-millimeter Walther P-38. That the Walther was never found. How two dingy slices of cheesecake showed up later to boost the alibi. I didn't reach the description sight unseen. There were pictures of everyone including the cheesecakes. They were so painted up they looked like draggers.

Any of these would have alerted a keen eye, but, what I was reading, it was probably more likely that surviving form of American tribalism: small-town politics. The Hatfields had their McCoys and the Sebrings had their Kantrells. And their Kyles. A three-way push-and-pull that took in enough counties to make a decent state up in New England.

The Kyles were cattle, from Tampa to Havana. The Sebrings had their groves and the Kantrells were dairymen. I don't understand pastoral dynamics but it seems cattlemen and grove people and dairymen don't necessarily share the same philosophy on politics. Or anything else.

At the time of the murder, the Sebrings were in an odd-man-out phase. Maybe too much partying, skinny-dipping. Whatever, they were politically weak. The prosecutors picked and poked forever before ultimately passing. Circumstantial evidence, unflappable alibis, and election-year weather. The election fell in a Sebring direction. Sherman walked.

The Sebrings got real quiet from then on and Davis Cambridge brought his sheepskin and shingle to Orlando. Davis coming along nicely in Orlando, this association, that club. Red-hot and rising.

My eyes had had it. My mind was stuffed like a fat man on Thanksgiving Day. I was about to click off when I scrolled down. About 1982 a new, interesting grouping popped up. Child molestation: the incest case. Fancy stuff. I jumped in.

I came up smelling like the bottom of the outhouse. Fifteen-year-old Terry had told a teacher that her father came in her room and fondled her and masturbated. He had been doing

154

it for several years at that time. The teacher went public, out-of-town papers grabbed it.

Even though the Sebrings were in power again, this one initially got away from them. A couple more articles repeated the first, then one about how the case had been gagged on account of the tender age of the daughter. News dried up. Apparently somebody was leaning hard enough to be felt from Tampa to Orlando.

Next, a short one. Sherman Sebring had been misdemeanored out of the system. He pled to a lesser charge, the article didn't say what. Maybe jaywalking. The lawyer Sebring money had bought proved conclusively that Theresa Sebring couldn't have been Sherman's child. No incest, no foul, plead out. The fuck got reduced, paid a fine and went home.

You have to shove pretty hard to push me sideways, but this shit did. I think I was actually shocked. The feeling matured into something ugly, and I could feel the anger and bile and all that alpha shit rising, sticking in my throat like a chunk of vomit. I closed the program and got up and spun around. My legs wanted to run. I got out of there. Fast.

I wanted to get on the turnpike and drive a hundred and forty. I wanted to stick my fist through a wall. I wanted to scream at God. I wanted to ask him how this was art.

In the end, God and I continued to ignore each other and I drove around in circles. Around nice lakes with nice houses lining grassy shores. Happy homes full of perfect citizens, living perfect lives. The best cars, the best schools. The best for our team. Hoorah, hoorah.

Watch it, Sloan. You're not even making sense. You're just tilting at anything that moves.

No, just everyone who'd had a fairly normal childhood. Why do they get to grow up in a TV sitcom life while Terry lies in bed scared to death, the man she thought was her father's got his hand in her panties, him pulling a batch? Goddamn. Damn God.

It didn't get much better. I wanted to see Terry but I couldn't have looked at her right now. So I drove some more.

Well, Sloan, there's a peek at that motive you've been looking for. A little murder, a little soft incest all packed up nice and neat and quiet for years. Then Randy Brian gets in the attic. I wondered how good ol' Randy was. If he was dead yet.

There were a couple of pieces missing still, but they were coming on. I could feel them coming on.

Next play was the other side's. It was their turn, but I needed to press. Take it to their house.

Scrolling Terry's number up on my phone was nearly effortless. Punching the button to dial it wasn't. It took a good clench of the jaws to do it, but we had to talk.

Did she know Davis Cambridge knew her father and uncle? That he was involved in her mother's death? Mostly I needed an in. A shiny, happy reason to waltz into the Sebring brothers' life. Either that or a sledgehammer.

The phone purred in my ear until a mechanical Terry invited me to leave a message. I left one. Call.

I looked at my watch. Terry was probably sitting in a motel room fucking up Rachel Ratliff's day. Maybe done and heading back this way.

Ideas were scarce, which isn't a bad thing. It cuts down on decisions. I found my reliable manual address book, found a number, but then the phone buzzed in my hand. I punched it.

"Yeah?"

Nothing for half a beat, then, "Sloan? Mr. Sloan?"

I didn't know the voice; it didn't know me.

156

"Didn't your mama teach you it's polite to identify yourself when making calls?"

"This is Detective Moraes, Orange County Sheriff's Department." Oh shit.

I found some shoulder. "Hold on, Detective." I didn't want to be playing bumper cars with this wicked thing we call traffic here when I heard what he had to say. "Go ahead."

"Did you know a Randall Brian?" Did I know? Did?

"Moraes, I don't recognize your name so I guess you're new in Homicide. A bit of advice. When you're making calls like this, you shouldn't refer to the deceased in the past tense. It's a dead giveaway." Unintentional pun.

He was flipping through the manual for a good comeback. He wasn't having luck.

"Hey, Moraes, you know a Lieutenant Mose Booker?"

"Yes, but you listen to me, sport, I caught the case. If you have information about Mr. Brian, you better let go of it. Right now, mister."

"Save the tough shit for the crack boys, Moraes. Tell Booker I'll call him. I don't know squat now but by this time tomorrow I might. I'll call him."

He was stacking the counts on me when I dropped him. The address book was still open to the page I needed. It took me a couple of tries, the way area codes change around this fucking place. All the way from lovely downtown Lakeland: "It's your nickel."

"Cut the shit. You're talking to somebody's seen you so drunk you pissed the bed."

"That could cover half the State of Florida. Easy. How's life, Sloan?"

"Tolerable. I need dirt. Old dirt."

Tim Zoran was the guy for the job. Supposedly a full-time news hack at one time, but nobody could remember where.

He'd been in Florida forever. Came up to Lakeland from Key West for whatever reason. He wrote an article for *Rolling Stone* or *High Times* once in a while. Did some stuff for *Mother Jones,* though I don't know what. Tim had pretty much killed himself in Florida, stepping on old and bejeweled toes. The *Trib* in Tampa was the only local outfit around with the balls to run his stuff, and that was occasional.

I ran across him looking at the wayback one time. An article he had penned earlier was a summary of a case I had at the time. I ran him down, told him who I was, who I wanted, bought him too many drinks and got more info than I needed. Ask Tim what time it is, he tells you how to build a clock, but goddam, the fucking guy knew Florida's not-so-ancient history like a book. We drank too much when we were together for two guys who had nothing more in common than an attraction to dregs and a predilection to take a drink.

"Who's dirty?"

"The Sebrings."

"Ouch. You do pick your dirty with an eye for quality. Which adventure? I got a trunkful of Sebring."

"How about where does a guy named Davis Cambridge fit? In the Sherman-and-his-dead-wife part."

"Triangularly."

"That's what I figured. He was fucking Sherman's wife?"

"Him and about half the horny of the county. Her name was Jackie. Country fried Jackie-O. But yeah, she and Cambridge were put together on multiple occasions by the prosecutor."

"How'd he come into enough money to move to Orlando about that time?"

"I'd have to check my notes. Could be the obvious. What else?"

"Was there any physical evidence? Particularly fingernail scrapings, blood, vaginal samples. Stuff like that."

"Seems like. There again, I'll check the old notebook."

"You have anybody can see if it's still around? If there is any?"

"Maybe. Cash money."

"Hey, Dad, you know me. Spend your money like it was mine. I need the hit on samples bad. How about this: how were the Cambridges doing in those days? Financially?"

"Down. Their wad was pretty much shot during the Depression. They had a few bucks and kept their memberships, but by Davis's time the money was pretty much gone."

"You see where I'm going with this, right?"

"Duh, yeah. Somebody's rattling skeletons."

"You got it. So keep me on the qt. Curiosity thing. What's the rumor mill turn out on the Sebrings' daughter, Theresa?"

"Got tired of Sherman chasing her around the house and fled. No one knows." Pause. "Do you?"

"No."

"Too quick, Sloan. This is over, I wanna hear it. Me first."

"Tempt me."

"Okay, try this. This girl ended up pregnant. Maybe sixteen, seventeen. Went away to have the baby and never came back." There was more. Tim wanted to make me work.

"That's an interesting story."

"No it isn't. But it gets there. Two weeks after this girl leaves, Horace Sebring and his wife adopt a baby. A brand-new bouncing baby boy."

"That is interesting. Call me when you know something."

"Give me a couple of hours. Tops. If you've got the Sebrings treed, I want them, Sloan."

"I don't know who I've got, Tim. This thing's crazy as a fucking bag full of bats. Call."

Tim wouldn't need the two hours. He'd go to task, push, pull, bribe, call back in half an hour. Tops.

I dug in a pocket and found a card. I punched the number in, waited on a mechanical voice to give me several options. I exercised one and got a tone. I fed in the code on the card.

A short wait got me Sarah Lee. "Lee."

"Hey, cupcake. How are things in God's-ville?"

"Immaculate. How's your investigation doing?" Things were different. We were business.

"Good. You feel like being a backboard? I've been research-ing and need someone to bounce with. There's a cup of coffee in it for you. Lunch, you want."

"You're convincing me. Where are you?"

"Twenty minutes."

"Perfect. Where?"

"There's a Cuban joint just south of you. Know it?"

"Yes. With the funny sign?"

"Yeah." Caribbean Tropic had been bent into Caribbeen Topic by a neon bender who was either illiterate or inept. "Twenty minutes?"

"I'll have a table."

I dropped Sarah and spun my starter. Two blocks, I did a legal U-turn under a turn arrow, nearly got hit by a guy turning into my right-of-way. It pissed him off enough he had to catch up and show me a finger. I made kissy lips at him as I peeled off and caught the interstate toward Money World.

TWENTY-SIX

The cupcake had coffee going by the time I cleared the door. I leaned over and gave her a peck that got nothing back to make it feel welcomed.

"So, bounce." God, she was a good-looking woman. And to think, she once thought I was sexy.

The waitress came; my cell buzzed. I smiled for the waitress, a small girl more Mexican looking than Cuban. *"Deme un sandwich cubano y yuca rellena."*

"¿Regular o especial?"

"Regular esta bien. Gracias." I produced the impatient phone and punched it to life.

"Sloan's Discount Investigations." I was trying to get a smile from Sarah. No dice.

It was Moraes, the cop, again. "Okay, Sloan, I need you at headquarters. Pronto. I talked to Booker and I know who you are."

"Uh-huh. But you don't know *where* I are."

"I know where you live. Planning on going home again?"

"Not for a bit, Moraes. Look, I knew your guy, but I didn't kill the miserable son of a bitch. My number was in a book. Big deal."

"Don't get between me and my investigation, asshole. I got something for that. You bring your ass downtown. Now." He was the voice of authority.

"Same story as before, Detective. I'm busy. I'll talk to Booker if I stumble across something that relates to Orange County."

161

"No, no, no, I decide what relates to who. First charge: interference in. . . ."

I lost him.

The cupcake: "The cops?"

I nodded. "Yeah. Randy Brian got dead."

We traded straight-face until she said, "How long are you going to ride this?"

The phone buzzed again and saved me. I'd even talk to Moraes some more right now. "Yeah?"

"Sloan?"

"Yeah, Tim. What's doing?"

"You sitting down?"

"Yes, Tim, I'm sitting down."

"I did my story in the *Trib* in eighty-seven. Twentieth-anniversary thing on the murder. I got shut down second installment."

"We having fun on memory lane, or what?"

"Listen, stupe. Sometime in eighty-eight, somebody notices it's gone."

"What's gone?"

"The physical stuff, brother." Tim was hyped.

Several of my balloons popped. "Shit. There goes major motive."

"What?"

"DNA. They didn't have it in sixty-seven. Remember?"

"I had DNA in sixty-seven."

"No, Tim, you had a bunch of acid-bent chromosomes. Thanks for looking."

"Cost me fifty."

"I'll send you a hundred."

"I'll send you a copy of my new article. I cover slavery in the Panhandle. Eighteen-Hundred to present."

"Can't wait." Could.

162

"Oh, Sloan, something I dredged up that might give you wood. At the time of the murder, Davis Cambridge had a peace warrant out on our boy Sherman." Pause. "You there?"

"Yeah, I'm here. Over the wife?"

"Uh-huh. Went on three, four years. Mostly fistfights till Sherman showed Cambridge his pistol. That mean anything to you?"

It meant I got a new angle on this thing. "Yeah, Tim, but it's still out of my field of vision. See you."

I closed the phone. I breathed deep, shook my head.

"Bad news?"

"Yeah. I had a DNA angle on motive, but the physical ev's gone. Has been for years. Shit." I was back to zero. Maybe less. Maybe not.

"Come on. Tell me the story." I know I only pretend to be a detective, but I thought I detected a tad of sunshine.

"Okay, here's my version. Keep in mind it's bits and pieces from old newspaper articles and stuff my buddy Tim either knows or is guessing at. I'll be filling in the gaps with conjecture, you don't mind."

"Conject away, Sherlock."

"Mid-sixties a young guy named Sherman Sebring, lives outside Winter Haven, marries the county tart and joins the army reserves. Not a good combination. Wild crowd. Swappers, swingers, whatever. So Sherman comes in earlier than expected one night from playing soldier, runs across Davis Cambridge—"

"The lawyer? From Orlando?"

"Same. But he's not from Orlando. He's from over there. So Sherman and Davis show up at a bar and make a loud run at getting drunk. Sounds harmless except now I'm finding Davis and Sherman had some bad blood over Jackie, the wife. Known fact. My buddy Tim says this went back three or four years. Fistfights, threats, peace warrants. These boys weren't drinking buddies.

"So our boys are climbing in the bottle and Horace Sebring, Sherman's older brother, and one of the farmhands come in, see Sherman, take him home where his wife has been killed.

"He's heartbroken. Torn up about the whole thing. But the prosecutor had a nose and smelled something. Some circumstantial stuff was all the weight the county could produce. Sherman walked."

"They tried him?"

"No. There was nothing to argue against a damn good alibi. The grand jury never even got a look at him. There was semen in the vaginal samples but they didn't match Sherman. Not enough physical stuff to get a blood type."

"So she fought?"

"Seemed to be some sort of struggle. She had tons of barbiturates in her system but that's what people did in the sixties. And that should be the end of it. Everyone lives happy ever after, even six-month old Terry, asleep in the next room."

"Oh God. Your client?"

"Yeah." I noted she had elevated Terry from prostitute to client.

"So what happened to the lawyer?"

"He came into a big hunk of cash and moved to Orlando. About thirty minutes after the fat lady sang."

The pretty head was grinding it up. "Time-of-death establishment? What happened there?"

Smart cookie. "Money. The Sebrings' family doctor got to the scene before the cops. He set the time about a half hour before Horace happened by. The county stiff doctor got the body after it had been in the funeral home fridge for an hour or better."

"Convenient. Why did big brother Horace happen to drop by?"

"Good one. And nobody ever questioned it. He was looking for his brother Sherman." She'd get it.

"And Sherman wasn't due home yet."

"Bingo. More fuel: Sherman was a pistol waver. Had a German nine-millimeter. Not a common round at the time. The lady was killed with a three-fifty-five slug. In a bind, you can't find nine-millimeter Luger pills, guess what you grab?"

"Three-fifty-five. No ballistics?"

"No Walther P-38. Sherman had lost it on a fishing trip. It was supposedly at the bottom of the Gulf of Mexico. And when the Cambridge alibi came under fire, a couple of round-heels were marched out. The reason for their late arrival was on account of these two hedonists and these two pieces of well-plowed ground were too modest to admit they'd all been daisy-chaining at the lake house.

"The prosecutor was riding a crippled horse during an election year. The case sorta dissolved. Never really got close to the courthouse."

"The story ends there?"

I showed her I hadn't forgotten how to shrug. "That chapter. There's another tawdry little thing that popped up in eighty-two. Child molesting, paternity dispute, no big deal." I could feel my face hardening.

"Your client again, what's her name? Terry?"

"Yeah. She was fifteen."

Maybe it was my expression. She didn't want to ask. I saved her. "Sherman Sebring."

Eyebrows. "Her father?"

"No. Turns out he's not her father. He gets reduced to loitering or something."

"And goes home? Just him and Terry there?"

"Got hisself a get-out-of-jail-damn-near-free card. Terry booked after maybe a year or so. But wait, there's more. Tim says, and he may be a hack writer but he's a helluva researcher, that Terry left pregnant. Soon after, Horace and his wife brought a new baby home. He and his wife were nearly fifty at the time, with grown kids."

The almond eyes blinked, distracted, off somewhere. "The baby could be Sherman's. Horace took it because it was blood. Jesus, Sloan. This is freaking creepy."

"Tell me. And I still don't know how it all fits to equal a bunch of dead guys, but it does. But if there's nothing to do DNA from, why would the Sebrings care? The kid? Sherman being the father getting out? It's obscene but it's not inbreeding. And where the fuck does Davis Cambridge fit? Yeah, he coulda been bought, but why buy someone who's already involved with the dead woman? Already paid for? The more I find out, the fuzzier it gets. Help me out here. You're outside looking in on it. What's your gut?"

Cuban restaurants. Our food finally made it and most of it was warm. We ate in silence, me giving the cupcake some room to try pieces, her working hard at it.

There was a bit of food at one corner of her mouth and I fought the urge to reach over and dab it, pull her off task. The chow was decent but way more Miami than Cuba. I ordered us flan and more coffee and we picked on in silence.

Her face came up. "The real version goes like this. Sherman came home early, catches Cambridge in bed with his wife. Then what, a fight ensues?"

"Or maybe Sherman walked in and shot her. I think it was more like you're saying. Sherman's pistol waving, everybody's loaded. Jackie dies."

"Sherman and Cambridge freak. Call brother Horace. He

166

sends them off drinking, fixes the scene. Then what?" She was into it.

I showed her a face that said I was guessing. "Horace cruises home, picks up a ranch hand, goes to Sherman's. Sees the door ajar. Goes in and finds Jackie. Calls the family doctor. Goes to the bar to get Sherman, tells him the bad news about his wife."

"Good story if you had DNA. Without it? Who cares?" She had a smile joyous enough you could break it out at a funeral.

"That's my dilemma. Not enough motive for the body count. Cambridge is in there with no motive I can see. His withholding evidence should have limited-out long ago. Fucking Sherman? Who knows?"

I rubbed my eyes and then my face. "I'm going nuts here. What am I missing?" I moved my hands and looked at Sarah.

Rembrandt couldn't paint light like that. "Nothing. You're just trying to see it all at once. Separate everyone. Cambridge, Sherman, Horace. Cambridge and Sherman come back together. Neither stands alone. You can't separate them. Horace is the patriarch. Why does he have to be in there? I mean, covering up a family faux pas is one thing. But snuffing people? Why would he care?"

I grinned some admiration. "I think you've got something, sweetheart. Horace might not even know what Cambridge is up to. I bet Sherman does though."

"Makes you wonder what Horace would say if he knew." A better smile. A promise, a maybe in it.

A grin found my face. "I'll let you know."

"Horace the first stop?"

"If I can find him. He's the only one worth betting on. It may blow up in my face. He could turn out to be up to his neck in it. If he is, I'm in there with him."

Sarah was working her phone, locating a pen. To the phone:

"George, two phone numbers and addresses. Between us only. Horace and Sherman Sebring. Polk County, Highlands County locales." Pause. "Okay." To me: "I'm on hold. You need me to get your back?"

A question I'd never had asked by someone I'd bedded. "I think I'm cool with Horace."

It got me a stern look. "Duncan, don't underestimate these people. They seem comfortable with disposing of problems with pretty extreme methods."

At some point we had passed over to being kinda sorta okay again. I didn't see it happen but I didn't question it. "I'm not underestimating."

Sarah's head wagged almost imperceptibly and I got some slight admonishment from the eyes. "No, you're looking forward to it. Aren't you?"

The need arises, I can lie like a three-dollar pregnancy test. Maybe I should have. "Yeah."

Our eyes held. "This is another part of you I'm not sure I like, Duncan."

"Me either, cupcake."

"Are you showing me these things intentionally?"

"I think so." Which was really no answer.

"Is there much more show-and-tell?"

"Some."

"Why are you doing it?"

"I don't know. Something I see in you. Nobody I've ever slept with knows what I do. All of it."

I was getting a nice smile on a nice face. "Is that exciting to you?"

"I don't know what's up with that, cupcake."

TWENTY-SEVEN

Those moments of clarity. The nirvana we seek in my trade. Bang. It's on you; you've got it. Any puzzle, even the most convoluted, will only play one way. This one was no different and I had it.

Thanks, cupcake. Horace was the man I needed to see about this dog. It was going to be a very enlightening day for Horace Sebring. Maybe for me too, but I thought I had most of the surprises worked out.

I was using the interstate in a Tampa direction and peeled off at Highway 27. I'm sure it has some folksy, sentimental name, but I don't know it. We do that here, we give highways cute, catchy names like they were our friends. Considering Florida's economic base, I guess they are. Considering the number of tourists that forget to go home, maybe we just think highways are our friends.

The Hispanic voice I got when I called had English not too good. I have Spanish not too good. We finally shared a few thoughts: Mr. Sebring wouldn't talk; Missy Frances would be home soon; I could call back; good-bye.

Glad I had an address. Probably wouldn't need it. It's easier to find people in the sticks by asking someone. After a few misturns and one dead end, I did some of the asking.

An indigenous place with a gas pump and beer signs popped up. I parked on some of the dirt lot and went inside. I got nine suspicious eyeballs from five guys who weren't extras

169

for a *Deliverance* redux but close enough you could almost hear a pig squeal.

When I asked where I could find Horace Sebring's house, I got laughed at a little and told I could find it right where it'd always been. Go west two roads to a blinking light, go right. Three quarters of a mile go right again. Follow the wood fence on the left for two miles, big white house. Can't miss it.

My back got laughed at some as I walked out. I guess that's what I get for living in town and wearing shoes weekdays.

The dope on the big white house was straight up. You couldn't miss it. General Sherman did. If he'd ventured this far south, the house would have had to run and hide in the bushes.

A big white thing with windows and doors and balconies at appropriate places. As the style required, it had a wide porch that seemed to surround the entire. A slate roof oozed over to almost inadequate eaves. Green stuff shot up around it like water was free.

I parked next to some very tame azaleas on a circular concrete drive. I unfolded myself and pulled my shades up. For its size, Horace Sebring's mansion wasn't much more than a monument to mediocrity. A soft collision of a big pile of money and not a lot of imagination. A yawn.

A couple of well-adapted outbuildings had found purchase down a slope of grass. One a garage, maybe once a carriage house; the other a barn from a picture. Some expensive horseflesh scattered around. A couple of hands at the barn looked at me looking at them.

The orderly azaleas frailed out in the sunlight and let some tough little boxwoods take me to the front door. The sun had beat on the boxwoods until they looked like bonsaied oak trees.

Up the brick steps and wide porch were a set of doors that didn't come with the house but were nice anyway. I rapped on one, saw the buzzer and hit it.

My Spanish-speaking friend. *Hola.*

"Mr. Sebring, *por favor.*" I was hoping she'd recognize my voice.

She did. "You call?"

I nodded.

"Mr. Horace not see you too."

"I've got to see him. It's very important. *Mucho importante.*"

"No, no, no. No can see Mr. Horace today. Call Missy Frances." The door was closing; my foot wasn't fast enough.

I stood there for a bit admiring the architecture, running my odds on having any more luck with another go at the *señora.* The bet sheet didn't look good so I hiked down to the barn.

Nobody there seemed excited to see me either. An old piece of rawhide in a bent and beat Stetson and a plaid cowboy shirt squinted at me with eyes full of emotion like yesterday's oysters.

There was a sandy blond kid with him of about seventeen or so who had eyes I would have recognized in the dark. He was holding a bay thoroughbred filly's head while the cowboy worked on one of her feet.

"Can I hep ya?" The cowboy was being business; the kid thought it was funny.

The hand dropped the horse's foot and flexed his back before he stood upright.

"I really need to see Mr. Sebring."

The cowboy pushed the hat up and squeegeed the sweat off his brow with a crooked finger, flipped it off in a smart move. "Lotsa people wanna see Horace."

"Yeah? And whatta they have to do to see him?"

"Best thing is talk to his daughter, Frances. She takes care o' his business."

"She's gone."

"Sorry 'bout ya luck." He wasn't.

"They let you in the big house?"

The cowboy flinched a little; the kid laughed.

"Why, hell yeah. Why?"

"Because I want you to go tell him something real important for me."

"Yeah." I was getting a squint. "Wha's that?"

"Something that's gonna make him wanna talk to me. What's your name?"

"Earl."

"What's your name, kid?"

"Chris." Chris was having a good time; a wry grin said so.

"Chris, could you give me and Earl a minute alone here?"

The kid didn't like it. The green eyes flared at me. "I'm Chris Sebring. Anything you need to say, you can say to me. I'm allowed in the big house."

"I don't think so, Chris." I turned to Earl, said, "Whadda you think, Earl? This goes back to Sherman and nineteen sixty-seven. You around back then?"

Earl's eyes came alive some. "Yeah. Chris, you go to the house. Now, son." The voice matched the face. Chris looked at Earl, typical teenager stuff. Earl said again, "Go on up to the house, son."

"Yessir." Chris pulled the halter off the horse and put it on a fence post. He walked off, not saying a word.

"Good kid?" I was looking at Chris, talking to Earl.

"Yeah. Real good kid. So what am I telling Horace?"

Earl wasn't gone long. He waved a beckoning hand as he

came from the house, I met him halfway and he escorted me around to the front door. It surprised me when he knocked.

The *señora* answered and Earl told her Mr. Horace wanted to see me. She seemed to know.

Inside was pretty much what I expected. The *massive* stair was there. The parlor and living room set up just like Granny Sebring left them. The tour was sternly Victorian. We slid down miles of wood floors that somebody spent time waxing. I bet it wasn't Horace Sebring.

The wood went to Saltillo at a kitchen from an army base. We trekked across the mud tiles and out a set of French doors. Down more brick steps to an open, bricked patio. Bougainvillea on trellises shaded the area. It was dark and cool inside.

A large man who had gracefully shaved off what little hair he had left sat in a rocking chair. He and the chair were about sixty-five each. He could have been older and so could the chair.

He wore khaki clothes, and a better Stetson than the farmhand's lay on the table. He had on work boots and he had rough hands. He'd spent some time outdoors, and didn't look like he'd be scared of a day's work.

"All you had to say was Sherman and Davis was up to somethin'. You didn't have to tell the help they was fixin' to get throwed in prison." He owned a pair of clear gray eyes; he locked them on me.

"How about if I'd told him they were killing people?"

He gave me a bold cracker stare, shouted, "Rosa!"

The housekeeper appeared and Horace said, "*Traenos cervezas.*"

When Rosa was gone I said, "That didn't get much of a reaction, Mr. Sebring."

"What's this gonna cost me?"

A hundred years ago, I might have gotten pissed off.

Anymore, I just grin. "Probably your brother. Davis Cambridge, if he's a friend."

"He's no friend of mine. We do some business. You gotta name? And sit down."

"Sloan." I used a wrought iron chair.

"I'm looking and I don't see anything that says you're law enforcement."

"I'm not."

Horace Sebring nodded slowly while he inventoried me. "So what's your asking price, Mr. Sloan? Let's get on with it." He leaned back, weary. Everybody had a price.

"I've been paid. Well paid." That earned me a look across his eyes.

"Awright, I'll be curious for you. Why the hell are you here, then?"

"I need to find Davis and Sherman."

"So you can send them to jail?" He may have been taking me seriously but I wasn't making him nervous.

A katydid whirred up in the bougainvillea. Above that, one of the constant airplanes of the times growled toward prior commitments. Above that, the solar system spun around our splendid, important little planet. Horace Sebring and I held our ground, held our stares.

"Yeah."

Rosa materialized in the stalemate. She off-loaded a punch bowl full of Coronas in ice and an opener. Horace dipped a couple out and popped them. "You sure you ain't looking for money?"

"Not today." It earned me a sweaty Corona. I blotted the bottom of the bottle on my pants, said, "Did you expect this thing to ever go away?"

Horace took a good pull on his beer. "Mr. Sloan, I'll not sit here and talk in riddles. You think you know something, you need to say it so I'll know what we're talking about."

"It's a long story. It starts in nineteen sixty-seven. Probably earlier. Runs right up to now."

"We got plenty of beer." His gaze wondered off, watching the grass grow. "Start talking."

"I think your brother, Sherman, killed his wife, and I think Davis Cambridge was there at the time. I think you did what you do—clean up Sherman's messes, wipe his ass. You gave Davis Cambridge some cash to relocate, and now you do business with him more to keep an eye on him than anything. You put it to rest but a newspaper article in the eighties started raising doubt, so you arranged to have the physical evidence disappear. To bed again." I stopped. Laughed a little. "I'm looking at you, you don't have a clue what they're up to, do you?"

"No, son, but I'm listenin' to every word you're sayin'. Go on, please." He opened another round. I didn't need it; he did.

"Up to current. Your niece Terry . . ." I stalled to let that blow by. He did good. ". . . had a car stolen. This gizmo she had in there called a Palm Pilot had a list in it." I was about to find out if he knew what Terry did to pay bills. It got him looking at me. "Somebody started blackmailing the men on the list." He knew what she did.

We sat in the cool of Horace Sebring's lair while he thought about these things I came bearing. I bet he could hear it coming like a train.

"Where do you fit in, Mr. Sloan?"

"I'm working for Terry. I was looking for the blackmailer when some people on the list started getting killed."

"Why do you suspect my brother and Davis Cambridge of killing these people?"

"I don't suspect they killed them." Well, maybe Randy Brian. "I suspect they hired it done. You people have any connections to Phoenix City?"

I got him. Good poker face, but he flinched ever so slightly. He also didn't answer. "That still doesn't tell me why you think Sherman and Davis are involved."

"I've eliminated anyone on the list who isn't in the funeral home except Cambridge. He's been spending a lot of time over here." Here it comes, Horace.

The gray eyes turned me loose and looked at nothing. "I'm having a little trouble on this list. Were these, what would you call 'em, customers?"

"Yes." Something was clicking.

"Why the hell was Davis Cambridge on that list?"

Here we go. I put out a pair of innocent hands. I couldn't see it needed saying.

Horace Sebring went red. Not like a schoolgirl goes red. He went so red, I got nervous. A few draws on the *cerveza* eased the color down. He cleared his throat like something was stuck in there.

"Mr. Sebring, I really need to find them."

Four beats. "If all you say is dead true, what would killing people on that list get you? Get anybody? How is anybody gonna connect blackmailing a buncha men on a list that belongs to a . . . Theresa . . . to what went on in sixty-seven?"

"I did. Maybe someone else did. Sherman having any problems lately?"

Before he'd lie, he just wouldn't answer. I could live with the arrangement.

"You haven't made it make sense yet, son."

The fucking guy was going to go cardio on me. "How about if you never told Sherman and Davis the evidence was gone? Used it to hold them in the ranks."

This attack, he went pale. A pause and a few swallows colored him back up a little. "You're still coming up short. How's this list gonna make someone dig up a thirty-five-year-old killing?"

I finished the beer, sat the bottle on the iron cage of a table. "Mr. Sebring, I've got the other piece. You do too, so you know I'm right. Where can I find Sherman?"

He looked at me awhile, then looked off across the landscape, his white fences and expensive nags. He shook his head. "Sebrings take care of Sebring trouble, Mr. Sloan."

"Mr. Sebring, you won't push me off. You may stall me, but you won't stop me. Bet on it."

"He's gone fishing in the gulf."

"With Davis Cambridge?"

This was tough on the man. "Yeah."

"You think that's where they are?"

"Hell if I know. I know I'm tired of secrets, Mr. Sloan, but that boy in there doesn't know about any of this. I'd like to keep it that way. Much as you can. I'd appreciate it."

"You gonna offer me money, show me your appreciation?"

"No. I'm done insulting you."

"Good. That case, I'll have another cool one with you."

TWENTY-EIGHT

I had a lot more in the car going home than Horace thought he'd given me. He knew Terry hooked, so Cambridge was keeping an eye on her for him. He didn't know Cambridge was a customer. Alabama rang a bell, meant something. He didn't give up squat on whether Sherman and Cambridge knew the evidence had been pinched.

What he didn't ask, what stood out like pink panties at a mosque, was why Cambridge should be in there at all. He didn't kill anyone. Horace knew. Secrets. The Sebrings were about nothing but.

The day had played out and I didn't have a clue where to find Sherman Sebring or Davis Cambridge. Horace told me where to find Sherman's house, but he wasn't there. The house was dark, not as well appointed or stately as the home place, but it knew Frank Lloyd Wright had spent some time in the neighborhood. Sagging beams and a redundancy of angular glass said so.

I hooked around and caught some six-lane in the direction of home. I could drop by, see if Mrs. Cambridge got those assets buried, see if Davis had popped by for a change of guns or something.

I could call Booker, the cop, tell him about means and motives and opportunities. Tell him I couldn't prove a fucking bit of it. Get a nice write-up in the local rag about how I was a fuckup. I passed.

My phone buzzed beside me and I nabbed it. The little green window told me it was Terry.

"Hey, Red."

"Mr. George? Mr. Sloan? Whatever? This is Rachel Ratliff."

"How you doing, Rachel?"

"Fine." It was nasal; she'd been crying.

"Sorry for you and the kids."

"Yeah. Thanks. Terry's been great. We're gonna stay with her till I can get it together. Our rent's way past due on the trailer and the landlord's locked us out. Terry wants me to work for her, housekeepin', and she's even gonna help me get in nursin' school if I want."

"She's got a heart of gold, kiddo. She around?"

"Uh-un. She tried callin' you for a while. A long while. You didn't answer."

"I was talking to someone. Is she there?" I was getting prickles up my neck.

"No. She had to leave. She said tell you somebody named Mr. Cambridge called and she was meetin' him. He was gonna turn hisself in."

We waited long enough, she said, "Mr. George? Are you still there?"

"Yeah, Rachel. I just can't believe it."

"I mean, that's a good thing, ain't it?"

Not this week. "And you've got her phone, right?"

"Yeah. Mine run outta minutes till I pay on it."

"Where are you?"

"Terry's place. The house in Lake Mary."

"Listen, Rachel, you don't go anywhere. You hear anything from anyone, you call me."

"You don't think he's gonna turn hisself in?"

"Not a chance, sweetie. You call me."

"Yessir," and she was gone.

The rest area came up and I slid into it, found a spot at the end that wasn't lit up like midday. I punched the windows down, killed the mill and sat there watching cars zip past on the highway. I might as well be here as anywhere when the call came in. And it would come. I wondered how inventive they'd be about setting my ass up.

An hour of getting out, sitting on a picnic table, the Wackenhut guy asking if all's well, me saying yeah, back in the car for a while. I don't wait well. Makes my ass itch.

A walk to the pay phone got me cupcake's message machine. I told her to call. Walked back to the car holding my cell phone like it was the cure for cancer. It didn't help.

A half hour it beeped. The cupcake.

"Hey, angel. You still interested in my back?"

"Yes. Are things doing?"

"Soon. They pulled Terry out."

"Oh crap. How?"

"Cambridge called, wanted her to hold his hand while he sang to the cops."

"And she fell for it?"

"It's how she wants it to end. The bad guys go to jail, everybody's happy forever. I need to clear this line. How about you bring any toys you can muster and come see me?"

Sarah said she wouldn't mind and I told her where she could find me and dropped the connection. And sat some more. Whether by luck or evolution, the mosquitoes finally found me. So did some other flying stuff.

I walked back to the pay phone and called the best midget lawyer I know and left him a message about a woman named Terry Sebring who had given me a retainer to give him three days ago. A thousand bucks. Call. He would. I walked back

180

to the car and sat in it, windows down, and fed the local flying parasites until I felt like Bogie in *African Queen* when he gets out of the water. I put the windows up and used some gasoline to run my AC. It got nice and cool and Sarah's nice cool face slid up on my passenger side. Her windows were down. I dropped the one between me and her.

"AC out again?"

"Yes. I didn't last twenty-four hours."

"Buy American. Come on."

She did, with a big canvas gym bag. Toys, I guessed. I leaned her seat up and grabbed the bag and stashed it behind the seats. Cupcake got in. Dressed to kill. I loved it.

Black leather pants, not tight though. A black fleece hoody over a close-fitting top. Hair in a single braid.

"Whatchu got in the bag, sweetheart?"

"The Ruger, the Browning. Small stuff. A collapsible twelve-gauge. Ammo. Flashlights. Vision aides."

"That should do it. All we need now is a phone call."

Another half hour, no phone call. Then, the phone call.

I looked at Sarah. "Let the dogs out."

The area code was where I had spent the afternoon. I wouldn't have recognized the other seven digits. It was a pay station.

"Yeah?"

Terry spoke. "You're not an easy man to find." Chipper. Off to see the fucking wizard in her ruby slippers.

"Where the hell are you?" I wasn't chipper.

"Settle down, Sloan. Everything's okay. I'm at a park outside Lake Wales with Davis and my uncle, Horace Sebring."

Something was wrong. "Where did you find Horace?"

"He was with Davis when I met them in Orlando." That, for instance, was wrong.

"When?"

"Three o'clock? Four?"

"What's the game plan?"

"Davis says it's my father, Sherman Sebring, doing the killing. Sherman got his hands on a copy of the list, and get this, the Sebring family has relations in Phoenix City. He took a shot at Davis yesterday, so we're laying low until we meet the sheriff over here at eleven." It all made sense to her.

"How close are they to you? Right now?"

"They're standing outside the car. Maybe thirty feet. Why?"

"Okay, Terry. I want you to put on your best face while I tell you something. It's very important that you don't flinch. *Nada.* Got it?"

The cupcake was looking at me like a cat, a big question mark over her head. I rolled my eyes at her and breathed deep.

"Here goes, Red. I was sitting at Horace Sebring's house drinking ice cold Coronas with him at three o'clock today. How long since you've seen Horace?"

Some hesitation, then a distracted "Twenty years. Almost." She was getting it.

An almost whisper: "Oh God, Sloan. I'm scared."

"Be cool. That's your play. Where's your purse?"

"In the car."

"Your car?" Of course her car. They had two bodies to dispose of later. Don't want to muss the family sedan.

"Yes."

"That little automatic in there? The one I gave you?"

"Yes, it is. Oh God, Sloan, I'm looking at him. It is Sherman."

I breathed deep again, reached under with my left and fired up the beast. "Where were you supposed to get me to come?"

"To the park here at Bok Tower Gardens. Someone would

182

meet you and lead you around to the lake house. That's where we were meeting the sheriff."

"What time?"

"You were to get here at nine so we could talk before the sheriff arrived."

"Do you know where the lake house is?"

"No, I don't remember. I know it's close by; I remember the carillon as a kid. You could hear it from the lake house." Pause. "This is so dumb. I don't believe this. I don't do dumb things. What do I do, Sloan?"

"Play the hand. I know how to find you. You get a chance, run. Don't stop. If you get your hand in your purse, remember the safety. Push it up and walk up to one, stick the bag in his chest and pull the trigger. Pull the gun out then and shoot the other one high, twice, then finish the first one."

Nothing from Terry, but Sarah was looking at me like the Antichrist was standing behind me.

Then: "My God, Sloan, I can't do that. I'll play the hand. Run if I can. Oh hell, Sherman's coming over. See you soon. Please." Then she wasn't talking.

I killed the phone, found reverse, then forward, and took it out on the tired old 'Vette. I didn't look at the cupcake, but I knew she was looking at me.

A half a mile I shot an overpass and did a fast turn and was headed west. I said to Sarah, "Buckle up."

I heard a click. No words. I let three hundred antique horses eat the road.

I used merge lanes a few times to jump blobs of traffic, but I used the emergency lane only once or twice and didn't hit a hundred until we cleared the attractions. On the grainy blacktop, after we left the concrete interstate, I reminded the car why it was made.

Not much of that, I was making the turn onto Horace

Sebring's road. When the lights of the house were in sight, I backed between rows of citrus trees and dialed Horace.

"Hello." A woman.

"Frances?" I could have seen her twenty minutes ago at the grocery.

"Yes." She was trying to figure out who it was.

"Could you tell Horace that Sloan's on the phone?"

"Is Sloan your first name or your last name?" She said it like it was a tad dirty.

"Last name, ma'am. I talked to him this afternoon and it's very important. Urgent." We'd see.

"You were the one who was here today. Okay. What did you say that upset my father?"

"Just asking him about old times." Come on, lady.

"About what old times, Mr. Sloan?"

"Ma'am, if your father didn't tell you, I certainly won't. Would you please tell him I'm on the line?"

I got lots of no talk but I could hear movement. A door was rapped, it clicked and, off phone, I could hear: "There's a Mr. Sloan on the phone. According to him, it's urgent. Or you want me to tell him you've gone to bed?" Then another voice not as close: "No. Let me see it."

More movement, then Horace to Frances, "Close the door when you go out, Frannie." A short wait, then, "Good evenin'."

"Evening, Mr. Sebring. We've got a big problem. You wanna save Theresa's life?"

I wonder what color it made him.

"I'll ask you again not to speak in riddles, Mr. Sloan."

"I just got a call from Terry. She was calling from a pay phone outside Lake Wales. Guess who was with her? Oh, that's right, you don't play games. Fine. I'll tell you. Davis Cambridge and Horace Sebring."

Nothing.

I went again. "You hear me? Hear me say she was with you and Cambridge? Going to a lake house."

I let him tussle with himself some and he surprised me.

I didn't expect Horace to tell me shit. I figured he'd play Big Daddy. Sebrings solving Sebring problems, didn't need Sloan meddling, thank you. So when he hung up on me it didn't blow my game, it just surprised me, made me grin at the phone.

"I guess we were through talking. You got some good eyeballs in that bag?" Sarah was loosening up some, getting over me telling Terry how to take two guys out with a small-caliber handgun. Considering what we were buying into, that sort of proclivity bothered me a little. Bothered my back.

"Sure. I've got a decent pair of night vision."

"Nah. Too high-tech for me. You got regular?"

Sarah turned and kneeled on the seat and came out of the bag with binoculars. I popped the lens covers and tried to tutor myself on adjustments. Sarah was viewing through a complex-looking lensed instrument, intent on the house. I didn't mind watching her.

She said, "Here comes someone. Large person. Big wide-brim hat. Horace?"

"Uh-huh." I raised my own binoculars. "Yep. That's the man."

We watched Horace mount a big Dodge pickup with duallies on the rear, could hear the diesel knock when he fired it up. Headlights bounced to the end of the drive and turned toward Lake Wales. I hit my starter.

At the first turn, I gave Horace room, but when we got to a stop sign, he was parked on our right in front of some parched siding with a roof over it. The roof had a few shingles. It might have been a house at one time.

I made the turn at the intersection, goosed it down, cut the lights and turned around. Easing up in line with the house let us see a wiry little man climbing into the truck. Earl, the farmhand from today.

Horace must have been in a hurry. He drove across Earl's yard, cutting a wide arc to catch the county road on to the east again. We eased out into his diesel wake, the stink drifting in a blue smoke.

The light at the only major highway was kind to me. Horace slowed but the light went green before he got under fifty. He hammered the big Dodge again. I came on, passed over the four-lane too fast, and bottomed out a little going through.

We passed through lakes and woods and a few groves, still heading due east. I let Horace have a quarter of a mile. The road was string-straight; I could've given him a mile.

"How does this go?"

I spent a few moments alone with the answer. If we weren't talking morals here, I didn't want to be the one bringing it up. I said: "Cambridge and Sebring think I'm meeting them at a bell tower. One of them has to leave to go get me. We take the house when there's only one bad guy there."

"Wow, Sloan, great plan. Divide and conquer. The simplicity is astounding."

"I don't really have what you'd call a plan."

"I figured."

Brake lights came on ahead and Sarah stated the obvious. I kept moving, rolling along about eighty, coming up on Horace fast. Earl was opening a gate to our right as we zipped by. I kept rolling.

TWENTY-NINE

A thousand feet, I geared down hard, cut my lights and found some shoulder. I looked around. Barbed-wire fencing on either side of us disappeared over the rise ahead. "Shit. Nowhere to stash the car. I guess we leave it here." I got the keys out, held them up. "You have to leave without me, these'll be on the back tire."

Sarah nodded. I grabbed the bag behind the seats and we trudged to the barbed-wire fence. Sarah knew how to cross a barbed-wire fence; she held it for me while the bag and I passed through. Then I held the strands apart for her. A cypress head loomed up and swallowed the private road Horace Sebring used. I motioned with my eyes.

When we made the edge of the head I sat the bag down. "What's your pleasure, cupcake? I know you've got that cross-draw .357 on your hip. The twelve-gauge?"

"Sure." Face intensely serious, nice bottom lip between rows of perfect teeth.

Sarah unfolded the shotgun, screwed the barrel in, and loaded it. She stuffed shells in her pants pockets like she knew what she was doing. My back felt better.

There was a little flat pearl-handled automatic that looked eastern European. It had been sanded and threaded. "The hell is this?"

Sarah glanced down. "I found that in the womens' rest room at work."

"Racy clientele. No numbers, threads for a potato. What is it? .32 caliber?"

"Yes. Shoots good for a toy."

Terry had my backup piece in her purse. "I'll take it." The little gun fit perfectly in the back pocket of my jeans. In a pinch, a funny gun beats no gun.

"You can have it."

"Thanks. What else do we need outta here before I stash it?"

"Flashlights."

"Good idea."

"Binoculars."

"No. We'll be in close enough we won't need them."

Sarah reached in the bag. "I'll take these." The night binoculars.

I shrugged and moved off; Sarah followed; the water seeping from the head made the ground squish under our shoes. No one was using the road so Sarah and I did.

The road was no more than two bare strips, twin footpaths really, raised slightly from the mire of the head. Sarah and I moved in nearly pure darkness through the coppice.

Sarah whispered something about using a flash. I made a sound, a negating grunt, just before I stumbled on a cypress knee. Sarah made a sound over there in the dark; it was an audible smirk.

Sarah tossed up the nocs, dropped them, said, "The trees stop ahead. We can reconnoiter there."

"Do what?" I knew what she meant; it was no time to be funny either.

"Jeez." Pause. "Case the joint."

"Oh." Touché.

The cypress trees petered out after about a hundred yards, and house lights glinted ahead and to our right, across open pasture. We held up in the edge of the trees, reconnoitered a little.

As near as I could make out in the dark, the piece of a road we were on ran across fifty acres of clear pasture. It dove into an orderly grove and continued on to whatever oblivion is beyond a Florida orange grove. Another three-stand barbed-wire fence sprung up at the edge of the cypress head and chased the dirt ruts on a ways then bent right or ended; I couldn't see to reconnoiter.

Sarah had the magic binoculars up, scanning, talking low. "Two people on the porch, the passenger still in the truck. The people on the porch are going in."

"That's gotta be discouraging for Sherman and Davis. Getting all ready to go kill me, and Horace shows up. What kinda vehicles we got, cupcake?"

"Horace's truck, the black Jaguar, an Explorer."

"Let's move up." We did. Along the fence line, the only cover we had. We held up at a clump of dog fennel, fifty yards out.

Sarah raised the binoculars to the house. I could see it clearly now. Flat-roofed ramble, screen porch across the entire side toward us. The promised lake was there, placid, quiet as if nothing at all was going on. A lesser road than ours ran from the house toward the fence we squatted by. I assumed there was a break in the barbed-wire somewhere ahead.

"Whoa." Sarah was coming out of a squat, crouching now. "What is this?" Her voice was low.

"What's up, angel?"

"I'm picking up people in the tree line by the lake. Two of them. Who would they be?"

"New hired help. I'm wondering what they are."

Sarah pushed the glasses at me. "Watch the trees over the roof of the Explorer. The infrared picks them up."

I could see two green glowing dupees, swaying around, bright dots moving like fireflies around ghoulish faces. "They smoking?" I gave her the glasses.

"Yes." She took them and leaned out, looking down the road.

Sarah moved back abruptly, said, in a whisper, "Holy shit. There's a guy standing at the turn-in." I froze.

"Where?" My lips made more sound than my voice box did.

"Down the road. The road to the house turns through the fence." A finger was getting enthusiastic. "Right there."

"Shit. Right there?" Right there was fifty yards or less. Maybe a hundred feet.

Her head bobbed. She offered me the lenses and I shrugged them off. The eight pounds of steel jammed down my pants was better for this. I pulled it out.

The moon was due but hadn't shown. Some laser show from Ratville bounced off the clouds but otherwise the night was a gummy pitch. I moved down the fence line on my stomach.

A rowdy group of palmettos had shot up tall in the sun. I elbowed for them and pulled myself into the little tunnel they formed. I eased up to my knees and peered out.

He was a heavyset roughneck. Hair sun-bleached so white it glowed in the dark. Skin tone only a roofer or fisherman could own. Twenty feet between us.

I eased back down and made a click sound like a baby gator makes to call mama. Thirty seconds and again. He moved a little in my direction. I waited. Click. He came in ten more feet; I could almost feel his eyes. He moved in, five feet maybe.

I raised the Smith & Wesson in my right about as fast as the minute hand on the schoolhouse clock moves. I put my left on my mouth and clicked, muffling the sound.

To himself: "The fuck is that?" He tried to mimic the sound, coaxing a response.

The roughneck stepped in and I could see his white rubber boots below the palmetto fans. You could have smelled him across Cedar Key. Muck island trash from the gulf.

He leaned close and parted the palmettos. He looked surprised for a portion of a second. Then I knocked his ass out.

I tried to grab him, but the shock of seeing me coupled with the smacking on the forehead, he tumbled out onto the double-rutted road.

I sat down. Ten seconds. "Raymond. The fuck you doin'? Get up, asshole." Another one coming over.

I lifted up. A tall skinny piece of shit with long oily hair under an oily cap. He had a shotgun that looked like it could have gotten him in some trouble about the eighteen-inch-barrel law.

"Raymond. You sleepin', asshole? Get the fuck up." A thud and a groan. I guess he kicked old Raymond.

I squatted, kneeled, then went flat, looking under the palmettos. Greasy was kneeling, striking a lighter, saying, "Goddam, son. The fuck you do to your head?"

Greasy sat limp Raymond up but it wouldn't take. Poor, limp Raymond. Greasy looked around, hooked his hands under Raymond's arms and began dragging Raymond, turning him, backing in my direction.

I worked my way back to a crouch, saw the back of a ropy head of hair and stood. I swung the gat again. Greasy fell into the palmettos so fast I had to sidestep like a matador.

The fence line got me back about halfway to Sarah. I risked it. "Psst. Cupcake."

191

She scrambled up in the bramble. Her expression was so serious I smiled.

"I've got two sedated in the bushes but have no idea what to do with them."

"Who are they?"

I wagged my head over a stretched mouth. "They look like gulf trash. Barrier island boys. You got any rope in the utility belt, Batgirl?"

"No, but I have plastic ties in the bag. Should I get them?"

"Yeah. And take these high-quality firearms and toss them in the mud somewhere, would you?"

Sarah said she would, took the sawed-off and the throw-down and skittered off in one direction. I did the same in the other. Greasy was lying across a palmetto, his eyes open, feet tangled, when I got back to him. He was as excited as a shotten haddie. Raymond was still catching up on his sleep.

Greasy had some beady dark eyes that began following me in a bit. I grabbed his scattergun and found a Saturday night special in Raymond's pants.

"What's your name?"

Nada.

"Whatever. You make so much as a peep, I'll kill you. Are you up and running enough to understand that?"

Nada.

"Want me to just go ahead and knock you the fuck out again?" I leaned over him, gat back.

"No."

"Good. We're communicating. Sit your ass up here." He did as he was told. "How many of you are there?"

He looked at me like I'd asked if I could fuck his sister. "I ain't gone tell you shit. Smell the coffee, fool."

I put the toe of my boot in the center of his back about three inches below the wings, hard enough to knock the breath out of him. I stuck his face in the sand and put a foot on his neck. Sarah showed. Perfect timing.

"What the hell are you doing?"

"Trying to get a head count." Greasy started coughing in the sand, making funny sounds.

"Isn't that a little extreme?"

"Sure, but I write it off against the extreme of getting dead." I moved my foot and the skinny guy rolled over, spitting sand.

"There's two more of us. The two old guys and the woman inside. Another guy just got here, and there's somebody sittin' in the truck."

"The woman okay?"

"Yeah. They got her handcuffed to a chair."

"The other two guys in the woods on the other side?"

"Uh-huh."

"Cupcake, put your piece on my friend here while me and him drag Raymond off a ways."

We got Ray to the cypress trees and I asked Greasy, "You wanna be gagged, make sure you don't yell out? All I got's my sock to poke in there." A whole different angle on being gagged.

"Nah. We can be quiet."

"Good. Back up to this tree for me."

The boys seemed pretty secure and we moved up to the break in the fence, about forty yards from the house. There were several spots we could have advanced to, but while I was deciding, things changed.

THIRTY

Yelling and scuffling from the house. The little cowpoke popping his door, not getting out though. Somebody yells: "Earl." A shot. The cowpoke is out, running to the house; two figures emerge from the trees beyond, running for the house also.

Sarah jumped to go but I held out a hand. "Not yet."

The cowpoke cleared the screen door and someone coming through the house door shot him and he went down. The figures from the woods went up the steps, onto the porch. The screen door banged.

Their voices weren't audible enough to catch the words being tossed around. The two hirelings lifted the little cowpoke to his feet. He pushed the two off and stood holding his side and spoke to them loudly. The one on his left had a long gun and racked it in the cowpoke's back. The cowpoke went down to his knees, then up, going at the guy who hit him. The other guy hit him over the head with a handgun.

It didn't knock the little rooster out, but he quit cutting up. All four men on the porch went inside.

The cupcake was mesmerized. Locked in a semicrouch, the Browning High Power had come from somewhere and was in her hand, flat like a ghetto thug would hold it. She broke her gaze loose and looked at me. "What happens now?"

My watch face was invisible. "What time is it?"

Sarah squeezed her watch. "Eight-thirty-five."

"Pretty soon here somebody, I expect Cambridge, will go

to the park to meet me." I thought about it, how I'd do it. "They'll probably plan on taking me at the main gate. We pull off the road, Cambridge opens the gate, goes through. I follow. Get out to close the front gate. Pop pop. Hmm." I thought about the time. "Come on. We need to beat feet."

Sarah and I jogged to the trees, found the two goobers where we'd left them. Raymond was awake and scared.

"Cupcake, either one of these blobs of pelican shit so much as breathes when that car goes by, kill both of them."

Both boys were telling me no problem; they just wanted to go home. I left them trying to get Sarah to light cigarettes for them.

A half trot got me to the gate out of breath. When I was breathing good, I sparked a butt and looked the landscape over. The bush wasn't much; a big oak tree by the gate sucked up most of the juices. The tree was too big to reach around even if you had gorilla arms. I stepped behind it, finished my smoke.

They'd blow a few minutes looking for the two lost boys, then go on, figuring the missing goofs had come up short on nerve and hiked out. I hoped.

Five minutes, I saw lights bouncing up and down before I heard the motor. The Explorer came into momentary view, then was behind the tree. Doors opened. Feet were on the ground. Someone still in the truck spoke inaudibly. A voice outside the truck said, "Yeah, yeah. We got it. See ya." Doors closed.

I could hear the gate chain clink, then the gate squeaking open. The motor revved and the truck was gone. Gate squeak, chain clink. Patience.

"The hell you reckon happened to Raymond and Edsel?"

"On't know." That one really didn't care.

"Well, they lose their share."

"Hell yeah, they do."

The sound of a motor and white light preceded "Asshole's comin' back."

The Explorer appeared, moving pretty well in reverse, backup lights working fine. It stopped and the horn honked. I could hear the trolls snickering on the other side of the tree.

"Go see what he wants."

"Fuck 'im. He knows how to get out."

He did. I couldn't see much of him but he was in a green jumpsuit thing. His shrill cracker voice gashed up the night. "Look heah. You come out on the paved road and look right, they's a car parked down a couple o' hundred yards. How 'bout one o' you boys goin' an' check it out for me?"

A troll voice said: "Why's that a problem? Somebody's car broke down. People's cars break down all the time."

"This one's got an Orlando tag on it." The way he said Orlando, it could have had an *r* on the end. Nobody responded. Nobody got it. "The boy we waitin' on's from Orlando." Pause, then: "An' long as I'm payin', I expect you boys to do what you told."

"Awright. Edgar'll go check it."

From Edgar, low: "Fuck you, hoss. I ain't checkin' shit."

Cambridge was gone again.

"You heard the man. Go check the car."

"Fuck you. You go check."

"I tole 'im you was doin' it."

"Fuck both of you. I'm rollin' a doobie." Rustling noises. It sounded like Edgar had sat down and leaned against my tree, keeping good on the threat.

"You motherfucker."

"Hey, I'll smoke this walking down to the car, or *we* can smoke it when you get back. It don't make a shit to me."

"Asshole. Don't you fuckin' smoke that 'fore I get back. You hear?"

Nothing, then, "I hear," as someone walked away. Then lower to himself, "You better shake it then, hoss." A little laugh, paper wrinkling.

I've twisted a few reefers in my life and never saw anyone do it one-handed but a one-handed man, and he didn't do so great. I eased around the tree, pistol first. Edgar was licking and sticking when I laid the barrel on his shoulder blade.

Edgar paused, joint poised in fingertips at his mouth, tongue out and moist. He cut his eyes across to me and finished twisting the joint without watching, a move he'd practiced plenty.

"Hold that pose, Edgar." I reached over him and grabbed a shotgun with some mileage on it. "Hey, cupcake, you out there?" She was.

The moon was up now and it was getting off enough light to see. Edgar must've been Raymond's brother. Same bleached-out hair; same dumb-fuck expression. He put the expression on me and the cupcake alternately a few times and ventured forth. "Who are ya'll?"

I asked Sarah, "Where's Tweedledee?"

She used the night nocs, said, "Still going through your car."

"Hold a light here for me, angel."

Sarah found a flash and shone it on my open wallet. From the selection, I chose one I'd never played before. It said ATF and I had to read the name printed on it. Joel Cardman.

I shoved it at Edgar, told Sarah to give him some light. He put the joint behind an ear and took the card.

"You read?"

"Hell yeah, I can read. What's ATF?"

"Alcohol, Tobacco and Firearms."

He was returning the card, "Oh shit. Ya'll are feds?" His face was hoping not.

"Okay, you can read. What's your buddy's name?"

"Felton. What ya'll gone do with us?"

"No telling, Edgar. You boys have jumped right smack in the middle of my party. We could start there. You got firearms; we like firearms. You got reefer; the sheriff likes reefer. There's also been a little murder. Everybody likes murder. You like murder, Edgar?"

"Uh-uh." He wasn't enjoying himself.

"What did you have in mind when the lawyer got back?" Edgar clammed.

"You and Felton gonna bushwhack the man when the lawyer led him in here?"

Edgar looked like he wished he had a lawyer.

"Just to let you know where you stand, I'm the guy's supposed to be following him back."

It got Edgar's attention.

"What'd he tell you I'd done?"

"Said you'd raped and killed Biggun's wife."

"Who's Biggun? Sherman Sebring?"

"Yeah."

"The man's wife died in nineteen sixty-seven. Look at me, Edgar. How old do you think I was in nineteen sixty-seven."

"Kinnergarten?"

"That's a little complimentary but close enough to make the point. You wanna go home, Edgar? Before you fuck around and shoot a federal agent?"

"Yessir."

"Good. Where's Felton, cupcake?"

The glasses went up. "He's about halfway back. How do you want to take him?"

198

"Edgar's gonna do that. Think you could talk some sense into Felton for us?"

"Yeah. Ya'll gone let us go?"

"Unless my section chief wants some of your asses for fucking up our investigation. The sheriff'll be out here soon. You and him can talk about the smoke."

"Man, that ain't lettin' nobody go." It verged on whining.

"Listen, Edgar, I got people all over these woods, glasses just like the one's the lady here has. See-in-the-dark shit. They've all seen you. I can't just turn you loose. Besides, you headed back to the house by accident, they'd kill you anyway. There's two sniper units out here somewhere. No. You go meet Felton. Get him to lay down his piece, you two walk back with your hands on your heads. We don't shoot unarmed felons in this branch of government, no matter what. You swing that?"

"Yessir. Y'ont me to go now?"

"Go, Edgar. You make damn sure we see Felton lay his piece down. Otherwise we start shooting."

"Yessir. First thing."

"Tell Felton I'm looking forward to meeting him."

Edgar was nodding and waving, then he was just part of the night. Sarah handed me the binoculars and I put up a hand.

"Nah. I know what'll happen."

She raised the glasses. "What? They'll run?"

"Like flaming jackrabbits. But I got twenty says Felton puts his gun down first."

"They're talking." Pause. "Felton's looking around." Pause. "Felton's putting the gun down on the road." Pause. "Hey, they're walking towards us."

"Give them a few."

"There they go. Oops. Edgar didn't make the fence across

the road. Now he's up. They're off. They run well in rubber boots."

"Lots of practice. Whatta we do about Cambridge? He'll be looking for Edgar and Felton when he gets back."

"You should've thought about that when you went filling poor Edgar's head with such mojo."

"How about we shift lateral, wait on Cambridge here, use his car for a free pass to the front steps?"

"Jeez, Sloan, that sounds frighteningly close to a real plan. I'm impressed."

"Me too."

THIRTY-ONE

The other two boys were ready to head home when I went back and cut them loose. I gave them the same ATF card and a similar line of shit I'd dropped on the other two birds. These two I told to just cross the highway, cross the barbed-wire over there and start kicking it. They liked the idea as much as I thought they would.

Sarah and I sat around for what seemed like a long time. It's hard to tell when you're doing this type of thing. Time does funny stuff.

She got up, stretched, and walked over by the gate. A muzzle flashed way off, the noise ripping the fabric of the night and sending echoes splintering off in all directions, and then Sarah spinning like a doll into the ground.

I pulled and threw a couple of caps at the night, the general direction of the flash and went belly first beside Sarah.

"Sarah."

Nothing but the ringing in my ears from dropping pills.

"Sarah. Goddammit." I dug in my pockets for the little flash I had. I found it, lit it, ran it down her body. Nothing gruesome on this side.

"Sarah. I wish you'd talk to me."

"You realize you've never called me by my name. What? I have to get shot to remind you who I am?"

"Angel, I haven't forgotten you for a minute since I laid eyes on you. Are you hit?"

"I don't think. I'm numb, but there's no blood. I think he hit my Ruger." She was doing well with this.

I raised my head and looked around. Nothing. "Turn over. Let me look."`

"Use these first. Locate the shooter." The binoculars were coming off her neck.

We were too low to see the muzzle flash this round, but the noise was there. The galvanized gate clanged like a bell and vibrated on its hinges. I knocked a couple more holes in the night, sight unseen.

"He killed the gate." I eased my head up with the glasses to my eyes. Nothing glowing. I raised a bit more. No bodies but a warm Ford Explorer parked down the road lit up. Cambridge.

I put the light on Sarah. A rag of material flapped at the bottom of her fleece jacket. I raised the jacket. The rig looked like an Uncle Mike's Sidekick, a tough little nylon holster. The end was shreds but the barrel of the Ruger didn't look any worse for its misfortune.

Lifting the holster showed me a nice hip line in pretty good shape. The leather pants would have a memory tattooed in them by fragments of the exploding bullet. A little blood.

"I should have been calling you Lucky. You've maybe got some shrapnel in your hip. You'll live. I'd be happy to check it out later."

I took another look through the glasses. Nothing was unusually bright then something close loomed. I rolled to my back and fired blind maybe three times. I don't remember counting.

Retreating footsteps got me to my knees. The glasses showed me Davis Cambridge moving into the trees of the cypress head, showed him disappear.

"Shit." I stood, sweeping an entire 360.

"I might get to like these things. They work on vampires and zombies, shit like that?"

"Give me a hand, you low-tech primate."

I did, checked her over again. Her face said the numbness was subsiding, but her mouth didn't. It said, "How did he get us?"

"My car. Ran my tag. He told me he knows people who wear badges. From there he figured what happened to the first two flunkies, figured the same fate would befall the other two and doubled back on us. He's parked a few hundred yards down. Fucker caught me cold."

"I can hot-wire a Ford." A flat statement.

I stopped. Man, she was from a Buick Six. Might've kept a loaded .410 under her bed.

"Well, Jesus, girl, let's go."

We did. Sarah opened a side compartment and got the jack and lug wrench. I watched while I repacked my clip. She stuck the beveled end of the lug wrench, the one for popping hubcaps, in the switch, held it through the steering wheel with her left and crashed the jack against it. Again.

The jack went over her shoulder to the back floorboard. She twisted the lug wrench back and forth, wiggled it free, wedged it behind the ignition assembly and deftly popped it out. She twisted it some and the truck came alive.

"You go, girlfriend. You driving?"

"Sure. Do I put it behind Horace's rig or put it on the screen porch?"

"The porch would be good if they didn't know we were coming. Get around behind the big truck as soon as you pull in the yard."

"I can stay behind it all the way if I go though the fence."

"This is true. Wonder what Cambridge has for a deductible on this baby."

That's how we played it. I sat the gate off its hinges and we drove through the cypress head and stopped. The cupcake looked at me, looked forward, hammered it and put us through the fence at about fifty. A few pops came at us. We could see them on the porch, two of them, moving down to get a shot through the screen. The cupcake adjusted to get us behind the big truck, but the side window behind her went away along with the back hatch window.

We came in too fast but my wheelwoman braked it out nicely in the sand. The glass in Horace's truck disappeared and we could see them. Spiderwebs began appearing on the windshield.

"Come on."

I scrambled between the seats and out the back where the glass had been. Sarah tumbled out beside me.

"Throw something at them. I'm going for Horace's truck."

Sarah peeked up and fired twice; I ran for a truck tire. Made it.

I put an eye around the tire and could see about six inches of someone's thigh between the low wood wall of the porch and where the truck body cropped the top of my view.

I put the Smith about three inches below the top of the wall and fired. I got a scream and a crash. A body fell to the ground in a net of screen.

There wasn't more than twelve feet between us, but there was a big-caliber rifle, scoped. Looked like a Browning 30-06.

Sherman Sebring looked like he could be Horace's brother. Same ruddy skin, same gray eyes. Not as heavy and looked like he was more prone to leisure than Horace.

He moaned and held the leg. He rolled over, getting it together, saw me and made a scramble for the rifle.

"Leave it, Sherman."

He thought about it, relaxed, rolled to his back and rolled back over with a pistol I'd read about. A Walther P-38. It was pointed at my face. I fired and rolled behind the tire. The tire exploded and began to hiss. I could hear Sarah and Cambridge exchanging cordialities.

I watched the sky and humped my ass up, found the little automatic in my back pocket. I rolled the other way and fired both gats twice, rolled back. Sherman screamed again and I could hear him scrambling. I risked a peek. He was dragging himself with one leg and one arm around the corner of the house. It wasn't easy, not shooting him. Not a bit.

Sudden silence. I looked back and saw the cupcake's feet and fine round ass where she crouched behind the Explorer.

"What's cookin', angel?"

"One of them went inside. I don't know about the other one."

"He crawled off. Left us all his guns. He's outta play."

"Hey, out theah." It was Cambridge. "Look heah what I got."

I looked. Davis Cambridge was behind Horace, a gat in the bigger man's ear. I couldn't see more than the smaller man's eyes over Horace's shoulder. Cambridge maneuvered a compliant Horace to stand in the doorway.

Horace was bent in pain, limping. There was blood on both sides of his pants leg and a towel tied around it. He'd been shot clean through but wasn't losing blood in bucketfuls. He looked angry. Maybe more bothered.

"The woman and the farmhand's inside. Ya'll gone back off, an' me an Horace is gone walk to that black car. You heah me?"

"The hell you doing, Cambridge? You're sixty fucking years

old. What? You gonna start new in Alaska or something? Give it up."

"I've done real well not listenin' to advice from riffraff all my life. You can save yours for the hoodlums you associate with."

My feelings considered the source and shrugged it off. "You're not driving out of here." I was bluffing, letting him think I cared if he left. "Not with Horace." That wasn't a bluff.

"I'll leave him at the gate."

"I don't think so. You walk him down the steps and to the truck. You leave alone."

"Awright. Ya'll back way off. Away from the road."

"We're moving." I scooted to the Explorer. Sarah turned and looked at me. "I'm dropping him when he gets clear."

"Let him go." Her face wasn't happy.

"Uh-uh." I was easing around to take my shot. "He'll kill Horace."

"Why?"

"If Horace is dead, who's telling the story? It'll be me and you and Terry against Cambridge and Sherman. In their county. He's gonna kill Horace."

I stood enough to see Horace's face and Cambridge's eyes, the top of his head. In the light behind him Terry appeared. "Hey, cupcake, check this out."

Sarah stood, figured the scene, said, "What's she doing?"

Cambridge spoke. "That's enough powwow. You're not gone outfox me so just move off to the trees. You don't, then I'll shoot Horace and go get the girl, shoot her. Then we got us a real Mexican standoff."

I guess Cambridge didn't see the farmhand worth negotiating over. Terry's full silhouette came in view. In her left hand was a cane-back chair, from that wrist a handcuff glittered, attached to the chair. Her right was in the soft brown handbag, straight out in front of her.

"Hey, Cambridge, how about we trade? I'll go with you."

Terry's hand was coming up with the bag. The safety, Terry. Don't forget the safety.

"No. We're gone do it my way. I insist."

"Have it your way, then."

The pop was no louder than a kid stomping a paper cup. That's all it takes, that close.

Cambridge stumbled, pushing Horace onto the porch. Horace moved aside and Davis Cambridge put his face against the door casing, stood there for a beat, then went down.

Terry put the little chair down and sat in it, looking at nothing, hand still in the handbag.

THIRTY-TWO

Horace Sebring was leaning against the wall beside the door, his hands on his knees, breathing deeply and steadily through his mouth. Terry was still sitting just inside, and Davis Cambridge was still dead in the doorway.

Terry turned when I came through the screen door. She had a laugh that choked itself into a sob. Then stopped.

Horace nodded the top of his head at me. "Good to see you, son."

"You don't seem surprised to see me."

He blew hard through pursed lips. "Frankly, I'd been more surprised not to see you out here."

"You okay? You're puffing hard there"

"I'm fine. I'm fine. Is my brother dead?"

"No, Mr. Sebring, he's not." I couldn't make myself sound glad about it.

"Where is he?"

"Out there somewhere. He's hit."

The cupcake crossed between us and looked at Davis Cambridge leaking from the head. She gave me a look, then stepped over the body and went inside.

I bent down and rifled through Cambridge's lower pockets but didn't find a funny little key. I found it in the breast pocket of his jumpsuit. I stepped over him and into the house.

The lake house was a main room arrangement. Cooking, dining, living lumped into a nucleus that fed bedrooms and a

208

bath off that. The centerpiece was a table about the size of the *Queen Mary,* stained dark from years of assault by baked beans and coleslaw and hush puppies.

Sarah was talking to the tough little cowpoke, him pressing a towel to a side, blissful for the attention from such a dish and one who had all her teeth. He lay on a plaid couch that looked like a little blood wouldn't hurt it.

I knelt down next to Terry and took her wrist in my fingers and lifted it. I used the key on the cuffs and they fell away with a clattering noise to hang from the cane chair. "How you doing, Red?"

She was staring in the direction of Sarah and Earl, but I don't think she was seeing them. "Is it over, Sloan?"

There was a pop in the dark and it made Terry jump. It was a sound I recognized. Someone had dropped a 9-millimeter cap. I was waiting on it.

"Yeah, sweetheart, it's over." I reached across her and brought the handbag to me, slid it off her hand. The little automatic I'd lent her was still in the hand, her finger still on the trigger. I pushed the safety to a better mode and turned the little piece out of her fingers.

I kissed her hand, kissed her cheek, rose and went out, stepping over Davis Cambridge again. He didn't seem to mind all the stepping-over he was getting.

Horace was gone. I knew he would be. I knew if I looked down, I would see Sherman's rifle, but his Walther would be gone.

As I turned to go back in, Horace came from the dark, Sherman's Walther hanging in his hand. I stopped. Our eyes met and I tried to put nothing in mine. You could have written a book on his.

"Sebrings take care of Sebring troubles." Nobody had anything that could hold hands with that. We held our positions for a few, then Horace added, "But I do appreciate your steppin' in. I owe you."

"No you don't. You don't owe me; I don't owe you. I'll give you a minute, then we need to figure out how this ends."

"Now you're lookin' down your nose at me. Maybe you think I oughta done somethin' a long time ago. Done somethin' about Theresa instead of cuttin' her off. You couldn't understand. You couldn't know how it is being a Sebring."

I laughed though my nose, a sound coming straight from cynicism. "You know, you're not the first rich people I ever dealt with. And I've noticed you've all got one thing in common. Want me to tell you about my observations?"

"I expect you're gone tell me, whether I do or not."

"You're right. You all think you've got the market cornered on money and morals. The money part, you're dead on. But see, Mr. Sebring, we've all got the same little set of noble ethics to sully. We've all got bones to break. We've all got skin to bruise and scrape. And trust me, when we fall down, we bleed just like you. And when you cross the line and fall from grace, you get just as dirty as we do. There aren't special rules; you people just fool yourselves into thinking so." I'd said it; I let it go, went back inside.

Terry had moved to the table. A coffee mug and a bottle of Canadian whiskey were in front of her. Her hands were around the mug but she wasn't drinking.

Sarah had Earl on his side. Antiseptics and bloody gauze lay around. She was kneeling beside the couch applying duct tape to Earl's side.

"Earl, it's gonna hurt worse taking off that duct tape than it did getting popped."

Terry turned, noticing me, smiled an odd smile. Earl looked over his shoulder in my direction. "Tha's what I tole the lady."

"And you know what I told him?" Sarah was still intent on her taping job.

"Shut up and roll over?"

"Close enough. How are things outside?"

"Stable. Earl gonna be able to travel?"

"Hell yeah, I can travel. Ain't nothin' more'n a scratch. I'm just enjoyin' the sympathy. You wanna hand me my drank, darlin'?" Darlin' handed Earl a coffee mug like the one in Terry's hand.

"I see you found anesthesia."

"Yes." Sarah turned on her knees to face me. "It looked like we all needed it." Her head tilted in Terry's direction, her eyes cutting that way, deadpan draping her face.

I had a little half nod for her. The mime acts were for no one. Earl was facing the other way and Terry was out around Pluto somewhere.

I walked over and slid a chair out and used it. Terry's eyes locked on me, looking at me, but on through me. The cup was empty; I put two inches in it.

"You need ice with that?"

Terry's eyes went to the cup. "No." She lifted it to her lips and took about half of it. It nearly gagged her but it put some color back in her cheeks.

I scooted my chair close and took her hands in mine. The eyes were the forest again, a hundred miles deep.

"It's over. All of it. You hear me? Over. *No mas.* The bad guys are gone."

"It won't ever be over. It's too late."

"It's over unless you don't want it to be. Your call, Red."

"I can't see it, Sloan. I don't see how."

"Horace might have some ideas about that. He's not one of the bad guys."

The eyes were emeralds. "I can't talk to him." She looked away. "What does he want to talk about?"

"About Chris. About a lot of things eventually. For God's sake, Terry, talk to the man."

The eyes swung back on me. They were aquamarine.

"Last train out, sweetheart. Don't miss it."

Her breath quivered in her nostrils and she nodded. "Thank you, Sloan."

"Don't thank me until you talk to Horace."

I got the nod again as she put the whiskey to her lips.

In a bit, Terry got her color back and her legs under her and we moved Earl to her car, packed him in the backseat. Horace sat on a picnic table under a light on a tall pole, the pistol on the table beside him. I walked over and talked to his back.

"Hey, I was rough on you back there. I think about Terry and the shit she's had to endure, I get edgy enough to kick a hole in the side of the planet."

"No need apologizing. You were right. I thought Sherman was worth saving. Because he was a Sebring." He shook the bald head, eyes on the ground. "I cut down the wrong tree. You gonna tell her?"

"What? That Davis Cambridge was her father? Why? Who does that help? I don't even know for sure he was. Do you?"

He was nodding. "He was." He turned to face me. Some quiet tears had passed earlier. Now he was stony-eyed. "He knew I'd kill him, ruin him, do something, if I found out he was. . . ." He wagged his head again, breathed deeply. "Goddam, son, the things people can do." He looked at me, showed me his disbelief. His eyes glistened.

"How'd he draw Sherman in?"

"Mr. Sloan, Sherman wasn't real quick. Davis Cambridge

212

was. Davis always could maneuver him around. Did it since they were boys. Maybe told him Jackie's death was gonna come back to bite him. Scared him? Who knows? Maybe Sherman knew it all." A rough hand rubbed at sun-ruined cheeks, brushing at tears.

"Who knew the people in Alabama?"

"Sherman. We got relations in Opa-locka that know some folks down the river. Sherman enjoyed threatenin' people with getting the Dixie on their asses." He exhaled. "Goddam, whatta mess. What're we lookin' at doin'?"

I shrugged. "We call the cops, they try to figure out who shot who out here, who shot who in Orlando." I pressed a piece of a shrug on him. "And you and I see it all and are still guessing for the most part at what we *think* went on." My hands came out, perfecting the shrug. "We've got two bodies and two more gunshot wounds. I don't have resources to cover that type of thing." I bet he did.

"I do. Last anybody heard, Sherman and Davis was goin' fishing at Crystal River. I'd just as soon leave it there." He nodded. "Yeah, I could arrange that."

"Fine. If I get in a pinch, you may see some cops though."

He didn't care. He ate cops; he wasn't hungry, he got the top cop to eat them on his behalf. "I'll take care of my end."

"I'm sure you will." I reached over and took Sherman's pistol from the table. "How deep is that lake?"

"Spring fed."

"Excuse me a minute."

The lake was a hundred feet down a gentle slope. A dock took me out that distance again. I looked at the piece of craft in my hand. Beautiful. Innocent. Inanimate. I tossed it as far as I could and made the moon's reflection ripple. I pulled out the little auto Terry had used on Davis Cambridge and sent it after the first. It didn't make me feel a damn bit better.

213

As I approached Horace, he said, "'Preciate that. Listen, Mr. Sloan, I know you don't think highly of folks in my tax bracket, but I'd take it as an honor if you'd slip by and sit under my bougainvillea and have a Mexican beer with me sometime."

"I'll think about it."

"And tell her, she wants to come see the boy, she can. I ain't got no problem with it." He did though. "I've seen her at his ball games and such from time to time. I knew it was her. Her mama had them eyes. Change color while you looked at her. Her mama's was blue. Never seen women with such eyes." He looked at me, at my expression, said, "What?"

"You want her told, you tell her."

Horace looked at me and nodded. "You come by and have a beer with me sometime."

"You talk to her, I'll think about it."

Terry walked up, put an arm through mine. "Your friend says we need to get Earl to a hospital."

Horace shook his head. "No, we'll get him to the home place. I'll call a doctor. We ready?" He turned, his eyes unbold, roaming between Terry and me.

"Not me. I'm through here." Come on, people.

"I'd like Theresa to drive us, if she would."

I looked at Terry, eyebrows asking.

"I don't remember the way." She and Horace were looking at each other.

Horace smiled a little. "I believe between the two of us, we'll figure it out. You wanna give it a try?"

With no change of expression, Terry said, "Yes. I'd like that very much."

THIRTY-THREE

The cupcake didn't say much when I told her we were going home and Horace was going to clean up the mess here. I guess she was getting used to my slant on unnecessarily involving the authorities. I figured I'd tell Booker what I knew eventually. The homicide dicks in my burg have plenty to do without chasing rabbits on my account. What went down here was Sebring business. I'd let them take care of it.

There wasn't any talk on the walk back to my car, none going out of the groves, through the gauntlet of fast food, gas stations and orange sheds and the artificial light of civilization. We hit the interstate, she said, "Help me. I'm fuzzy here."

"Me too. Some. It starts out simple enough. The redneck jack boys sell the car and Palm Pilot to Grady. Grady figures Terry's racket, goes entrepreneurial and makes a few calls. Fishing some. Catches Randy Brian. Randy talks Grady out of the list, takes pictures, ferrets out these men on the list, digs into their lives. Then Randy made the connection between Cambridge and Sebring."

"How?"

"Same way I did, probably. At the public library. I expect The Brain was researching Cambridge, looking at club memberships and professional affiliations. Stuff to use for leverage. Up pops the dirty little incident in sixty-seven and the Brain knows he's got something. Maybe even calls Sherman, I don't know. Sherman plays the big shot. Gonna

215

handle the problem, take care of business. Calls Alabama. Brian sets up a money drop, pussies out. Grady gets popped."

"The men from Alabama?"

"I expect. They got all Grady had to give which was a copy of the list, Randy Brian's nickname and his life. Grady didn't know who Randy was, only that Randy was a customer of Terry's. *Chien,* the dog. I'm sure he gave them all he had on Randy and the crackerjacks too. Told them I was skulking around.

"In a panic, Cambridge and Sherman tell the hicksters to start going down the list. Sent them over to push me off and convince Terry to let it go. But Randy's still busy making phone calls. Probably set himself up like a bowling pin. The 'Bama boys were busy talking to Sammy B. when Brian fell down, so that one was on Cambridge and Sherman.

"Then I pop up again. Terry and I become loose ends to be taken care of. Cambridge draws Terry out. They knew I'd show whether I thought all was kosher or not. They didn't know I'd talked to Horace. Or that he'd get out there ahead of us. So it all went to shit."

I got a look that wasn't warm. "It didn't go to shit. You made it go to shit. And Horace didn't *get* out there; you *sent* him." All I had for that was a big shrug.

A few miles of concrete highway slipped under us and she said, "So Cambridge's motive was what? Keeping Jackie's murder quiet?"

"I don't think he gave much of a shit about that. That was just something he had on the Sebrings. He was afraid Horace would find out he had been keeping a closer eye on Terry than Horace intended."

"Loss of income? Wasn't that the majority of his business?"

"Maybe. It was easy money. A kinder, gentler form of blackmail for his continued silence about Jackie. But like I